Also by Kaitlin Ward

Where She Fell

Girl in a Bad Place

Bleeding Earth

LIE TO ME

Kaitlin Ward

POINT

Copyright © 2019 by Kaitlin Ward

Photos ©: cover girl: Michael Frost; cover water: Jovana Rikalo/Stocksy; interior water: Michael Frost; interior emoticons throughout: Iefym Turkin/iStockphoto.

All rights reserved. Published by Point, an imprint of Scholastic Inc., *Publishers since 1920.* SCHOLASTIC, POINT, and associated logos are trademarks and/or registered trademarks of Scholastic Inc.

The publisher does not have any control over and does not assume any responsibility for author or third-party websites or their content.

No part of this publication may be reproduced, stored in a retrieval system, or transmitted in any form or by any means, electronic, mechanical, photocopying, recording, or otherwise, without written permission of the publisher. For information regarding permission, write to Scholastic Inc., Attention: Permissions Department, 557 Broadway, New York, NY 10012.

This book is a work of fiction. Names, characters, places, and incidents are either the product of the author's imagination or are used fictitiously, and any resemblance to actual persons, living or dead, business establishments, events, or locales is entirely coincidental.

Library of Congress Cataloging-in-Publication Data available

ISBN 978-1-338-53810-6

10 9 8 7 6 5 4 3 2 1   19 20 21 22 23 24

Printed in the U.S.A.   23

First edition, January 2020

Book design by Maeve Norton

To the town of Monroe:
You will always be home.

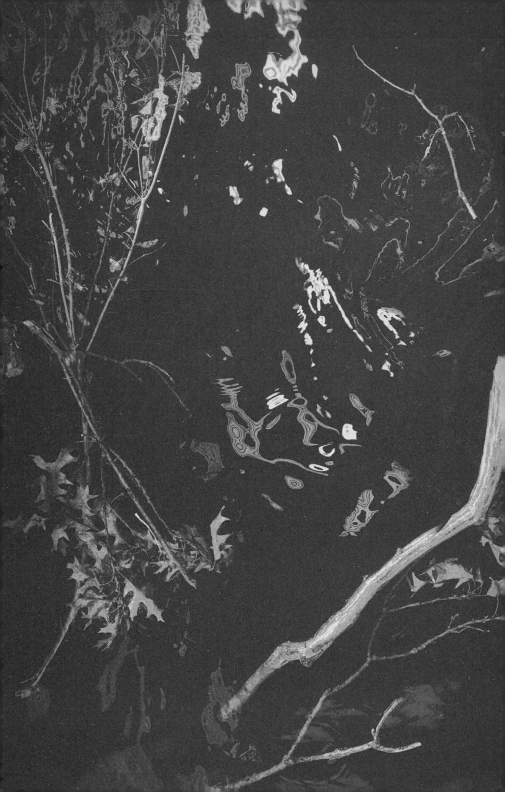

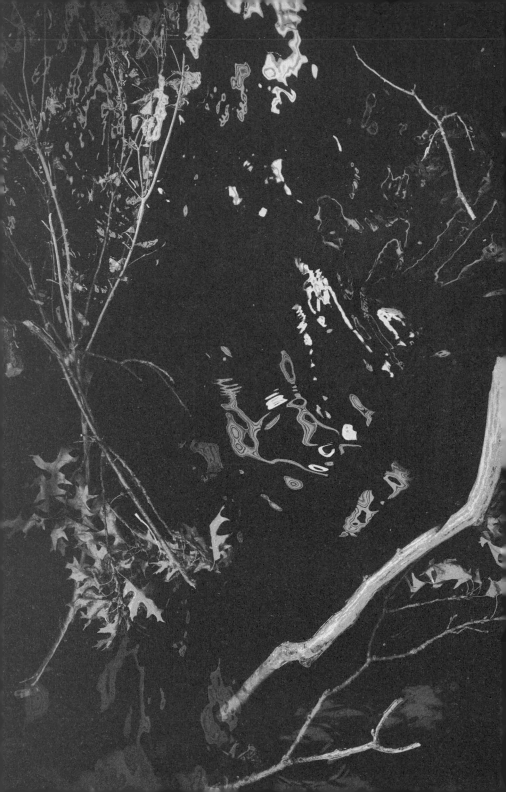

1

GIRL DROWNS IN PASSUMPSIC RIVER.

When I see the headline, I almost drop my phone. It's a link someone posted on Facebook from the local news.

I tap the screen with shaking fingers and read the article in a rush. A twenty-year-old college sophomore, Maria Lugen. Survived by both parents and a younger brother, Steve, who goes to my high school. Maria had been missing for a month. Her death is currently believed to be an accident. No additional information at this time.

I set down the phone carefully on my bed and go stand in front of the mirror hanging on my closed door. I stare at my reflection until my features start to feel distorted and unreal, like a word you've repeated too many times in a row.

Because what happened to that girl—it can't have been an accident. It's too much of a coincidence. I move closer to the mirror, stare at myself from only an inch away. My skin is bruised in places, and there's a cast on my wrist. My head spins if I stand up too fast. Because I hit my head and fell down an embankment, almost into a river. Unlike Maria, I survived.

But I don't think I was meant to.

"This seems like a terrible idea, Amelia." My best friend Skylar's hands are white-knuckle fists around the steering wheel of her Corolla. "Isn't it too soon? Won't it upset you to go back to the spot where you nearly died?"

"I don't think there's a *too soon* for this type of thing."

"Maybe not, I guess, but remind me again how this is going to help? I still think all this is going to do is upset you, and we should spend our time finding a *new* spot instead."

"I don't *want* a new spot. I want to have not almost *died* at the old spot."

She flinches, and I feel bad. Before returning to school this week, I spent four days recovering at home after three days in the hospital with bruises and breaks and a concussion. That last one is what worried everyone the most, and it's the thing my family and friends all still worry about. The concussion kept me from remembering exactly what happened when I fell, and it's left headaches and occasional vertigo in its wake. Sky wants me to focus on letting myself rest and feel better. She's not wrong, but she doesn't know everything.

No one knows that I suspect I'm in danger from a source other than my own brain. Not even my best friend.

I glance sidelong at Sky. She's supermodel tall, and thin as a spike. Her naturally blond hair is dyed a shade of pink that edges just close enough to "the natural spectrum" that our school doesn't make her change it, and it's cut into a short, layered bob. Her heart-shaped face is littered with freckles, and right now her jaw is clenched tight enough that I can practically feel her teeth grinding.

"I just need to see it, okay?" I say softly as the river comes into view at the bottom of the long winding drive down to the dam. No one else is here. Late September is not a super popular time for beachgoers. "I want to see if I, like, *feel* anything. I know how that sounds, but just bear with me."

Sky parks her car and cuts the ignition. "You know I will." She opens the door, then pauses with a small smile. "But the second you start using essential oils I'm ordering an intervention."

I laugh. "Deal."

We follow the portage trail that winds behind the dam. It's a collision of natural and unnatural beauty back here: The stark cliff of cement, and the rushing water at its base. The trees and the rocks around its edges, and the mountains in the background. It's a place I've always loved, and I hate that it's tainted now. I stop walking, press my shins right up against the guardrail. This side of the rail is a paved path, and the other side is a few feet of grass and then a long, steep slope to the water below. The brush is marred with heavy lines of dirt. Bushes have been hacked away, and tree branches have been broken. Some from my fall, some from my rescue.

This is where Sky found me. The last thing I remember is sitting on this guardrail, waiting for her to arrive. She had something to tell me, she'd said. Something important. And this was our spot. The place where we'd always come to swap secrets. My mind is pretty much a blank space after that. I remember the feeling of something pushing my shoulder, but I don't remember anyone else being near me. Doctors say I must have lost my balance after standing up on the wrong side of the guardrail. Then I fell, tumbling partway down the rocky hill and by sheer, unfathomable luck, I got hung up in a tree and didn't drop the rest of the way to my death.

My neurologist told me that I probably won't remember anything new and that the reason I don't remember my fall isn't because I've buried a traumatic memory but because my concussion means the memory doesn't even exist. I hate that. The idea that something can happen to you and can be completely ignored by your own brain. I want my neurologist to be wrong, and that's the main reason I'm here.

Peering down into the abyss below me, I get such an intense wave of vertigo that I have to sit down on the path. I pull off my new lime-green glasses and press one palm into my forehead between my eyebrows until the dizziness passes. I'm on the right side of the guardrail, I remind myself. The safe side.

"You okay?" Sky asks. She crouches beside me, rests a hand on my back.

"I'm fine." I swallow nausea, unwilling to admit that maybe she was right and this was a bad idea. It's just a *place*. I shouldn't have to feel this way about it. I replace my glasses and stand up, stretching my arms. My left one is heavy, thanks to the cast surrounding my broken wrist. It makes stretching a lot less satisfying.

And then I . . . *feel* something. A shadow of a past sensation, like something's tugging at my throat. My hand flits there, to where my favorite necklace normally would be—a rectangle made out of wood scraps on a thin chain that my dad and brother made together and gave me for Christmas a few years ago—but it's missing. Along with my glasses, I lost the necklace when I fell. Suddenly, I can recall a tightness against my throat, and then the sensation of absence. I shut my eyes and try to expand that feeling, remember something else. Something *real*. Nothing else comes, but still, I feel hopeful. Maybe the doctor was wrong, after all. Maybe I *will* remember what happened.

"You sure you're all right?" Sky persists.

I open my eyes. "Yeah. I'm just . . . thinking."

She perches cautiously on the road side of the guardrail, fingers curled around the metal. It's really not that close to the edge, I notice. Not close enough for me to have stood up, stumbled, and fallen halfway down the slope, in my opinion.

"Thinking about what?" she asks.

"What was the important thing you were going to tell me that day?" It's not the first time I've asked. She doesn't seem to want to tell me anymore, but I'm hoping maybe here, she'll change her mind—it's the *other* reason I wanted to come back, and it's the reason I wanted Sky to come with me. With the water crashing out the back of the dam, sometimes it feels like the sound swallows up your secrets and keeps them safe. That's why it's always been our meeting place.

"It seemed important at the time," she says. "But now . . ." A shrug. "I don't want to talk about it."

"But—"

"It's not relevant, okay?" Her tone is almost snappish, and it stops me from pressing the matter more.

We've drifted recently, or so it feels to me. Months ago, maybe sometime in July, I noticed that she was busy more often when I texted her to make plans. I pulled back a little, and I hoped that she would notice, but she didn't seem to. She is still here when I need her, so sometimes I think it's all in my head.

But it makes me wonder about her secret. If maybe there's something she wanted to say—something that was making her distant. And if maybe she decided not to because she feels bad for me after what happened.

I hope that's not the case, but I get a pit in my stomach when I think about it.

Usually, I would tell her about what I remembered. She might tell me that remembering my necklace snapping means nothing, because that's Sky: my most pragmatic friend. But she would also listen and she wouldn't make me feel stupid.

Except now she's keeping something from me, and it doesn't put me in much of a sharing mood.

"I don't think I'm going to remember anything," I say. "We should just go."

"You sure?"

"I'm sure."

She stands up, biting her lip. "You look disappointed, Amelia. I didn't want you to be disappointed. That's why I thought we shouldn't come."

"I'm not disappointed." I fold my arms. "I didn't have any expectations."

"Good." She hugs me. "And now we've been here and you've seen it, and maybe that's what you needed to just, like, move forward. Dwelling on what happened isn't going to make it un-happen, and it's better if you just don't think about it too much."

"I know." I smile half-heartedly. "You're right, Sky."

Except I don't think she's right. I'm not going to be able to stop dwelling on this. When everyone told me that this was an accident, I wanted to believe them. I *tried* to believe them. But I've felt it in my gut this whole time that something else hap-pened. Something much less innocent. It's based on nothing, really, except that I'm always careful and that something feels *off*. I told my doctor that the last thing I remember before it all goes blank is a sensation like a hand pushing my shoulder. I don't remember anyone *being there*, though, and my doctor dis-missed it so fast as concussion-related disorientation that I've been too embarrassed to tell anyone since. But the gut feeling remains, and after I saw that news article about Maria Lugen's death, the feeling has strengthened tenfold.

I don't *want* someone to have tried to kill me.

But if they *did*, I want to know who it was. And why me.

And I want to catch them before they try it again.

2

School has not been my favorite thing since my brush with death. Maybe it's a little bit of narcissism, but in the few days I've been back I just feel very . . . watched. It's not that I was an outcast before, but I was *regular*. There was no reason for people to talk about me or be interested in me at all, and I didn't realize how great that anonymity was until I lost it.

I've already spent way too long getting ready this morning. Everything takes forever thanks to my dumb broken wrist, but my newfound self-consciousness is also to blame. I tied my chestnut hair into a messy bun that *looks* like it took three seconds but actually took a half hour to get perfect. I drew green eyeliner across my upper lid and then decided that green eyeliner green glasses green eyes was too much and replaced it with black. I'm not sure how I feel about these new glasses yet. I tried on three lipsticks before deciding to forget about that altogether, and I'm just finishing up my mascara when Mom calls my name from downstairs using her Impatient Voice. I quickly drop the mascara back onto my desk and hurry downstairs, not letting myself stop to analyze my outfit again in the mirror on my door.

Mom's folded arms await me at the bottom of the stairs, and a plate of heavily syruped, A-shaped pancakes greets me at the kitchen table.

Dad owns a small trucking company, and he also drives one of the trucks himself. He's home most weekends, but the rest of the time, it's just Mom; my older brother, Hunter; and me. Soon to be just Mom and me, because Hunter's a senior this year. Mom does a lot of the management of Dad's business, keeping track of all his paperwork and his drivers, and she is also better at managing a house than anyone I've ever met. My aspirations are different from hers, but if I'm even half as successful as she is when I grow up, I'll consider myself lucky.

Despite this, the A-shaped pancakes are a bad sign. She usually only whips those out when she thinks I really need them. When I lost my first tooth. The day of my first period. Anytime I've broken up with a boyfriend.

Weirdly, I didn't get them my first morning back home after the accident. Or my first morning back at school. So what does it mean that I'm getting them now?

"Where's Hunter?" I ask, shoveling pancake into my mouth.

Mom sits on the other side of the table. "He complained about how long you were taking, so I sent him to clean the car while he waited."

I hide a smile by stuffing another bite of pancake into my

mouth. My brother is a complete slob. Serves him right to have to clean.

"Don't give me that smug look," says Mom, eyes narrowed. "You're not much higher on the neatness scale."

"Excuse me. I am a *lot* better. Just not compared to you."

That softens her expression.

"Mom." I pause, cutting the rest of my pancakes into pieces. "Why the special pancakes?"

She sighs. "Because I noticed you've been reading about the girl who drowned and I can tell you're upset about it, and I want you to stop."

The bite turns to dust in my mouth. I didn't realize she had noticed. I've been working so hard at pretending nothing's bothering me, but clearly not hard enough.

"I'll stop," I tell her. "It's just tough to think about, you know? Given that my circumstance was almost . . ."

"I know." Mom grabs my empty plate, takes it to the dishwasher. "It's tragic. *Heartbreaking*, to think about what that girl's mom must be going through." She pauses, and I can tell by the set of her jaw that she's fighting back tears. "But honey— I just don't want to see you dwell. Are you sure you don't want to see Hunter's therapist?"

"I'm sure." I shoulder my backpack and give her a weak smile. I would love to scrub this entire event from existence, rip open the seams of time and sew them back together without it. But talking isn't going to help—that's just not how I'm built.

I know the therapist my brother sees once a month is great, but I'm not going to solve how I feel about my near-death experience by telling her about it. In a different scenario, therapy would be the right choice. But in *this* scenario, I need to take action.

I'm just lost about how to even begin.

Murders aren't a thing that happens in Maple Hill, New Hampshire, a town of seven hundred residents, most of whom know one another in some way. Crime of any kind, for that matter, barely happens. The larger town of St. Elm, across the river in Vermont and where my high school is located, has more going on. But even there, murders are shocking.

So for me to prove someone tried to hurt me, let alone convince anyone else—or even, really, myself—well. It's not only going to be an uphill battle.

It's a cliff.

St. Elm Academy is a series of buildings laid out on a well-manicured campus, sort of like a miniature college. It's semi-private, populated by students from afar whose parents pay for them to live in dorms and by kids like me from the many local small towns that don't have their own high schools. We don't have uniforms, but we do have a dress code, and the skirt I wore today is pushing the length limit a little. It's been on my mind this morning more than I want it to be, especially now as I weave through the cafeteria feeling like there is a giant beaming sign over my head flashing *dress code violation!* I already felt like I had a *near-death girl!* sign up there, so this is too much.

My high school is not one of those places where sharp lines have been drawn between different groups. Not that there aren't cliques, because there are *always* cliques, but there is no harsh social hierarchy based on looks and extracurriculars. Still, some people are more noticeable, more *known*, than others—for both good and bad reasons. Because of my accident, because of the article in the local newspaper that got shared on social media by practically everyone I'd ever met, I've become one of those people. And I don't like it. I didn't used to agonize over what I wore or how my makeup looked. I figured if I was going to experiment a little bit to figure out what I like, sometimes my outfits or my makeup just wouldn't be that good. But now, every time I hear someone whispering, I assume it's about me. I know most of the time it probably *isn't*, but it makes me very aware of my face and my hair and my body. They all think I tripped and fell like some kind of moron, so I want them to see how put together I am. How not accident-prone.

Balancing my tray on my cast, I tug at the bottom of my skirt again. The tray tilts, not enough that it's going to fall, but a hand reaches out and grabs it. So much for not accident-prone.

"Careful," says the owner of the hand. And of course, it's Liam Hawthorne, my brother's "mortal enemy." Hunter's words, not mine.

"I had it," I say, cheeks burning.

"I'm sure you did." He lets go of the tray but stands in front of me for a few seconds longer anyway. I raise my eyebrows just slightly, waiting for him to say something else or move out of my way. Finally, he says, "It's good to see you back, Amelia."

"I'm sure you were super worried about me."

For a moment, an expression of hurt flashes across his face, but it's gone almost before I can register it. "I know we're not friends," he says coolly, "but whose fault is that, yours or mine?"

He leaves, and I feel like a jerk.

Liam is very handsome, tall and lanky with dark brown hair, bright blue eyes, and tanned skin. He and Hunter are both seniors, and they've led what was once a decidedly mediocre soccer team to the state championship two years in a row. But before high school, Hunter was the star of Maple Hill's middle school team, and Liam was his rival in Hen Falls. They've never been able to move past that old rivalry, at least not off the field. And I'm a loyal sister, so I'm obviously Team Hunter. But as I watch Liam walk away, I think it's too bad they can't figure out how to get along. Liam seems like a perfectly nice guy, but he's guarded and a little isolated. He isn't enemies with the rest of his team like he's enemies with Hunter, but they're not exactly clamoring to hang out with him, either. I've never understood it, personally.

"Making new friends, I see?" teases Sky when I set my tray down across from her at the table where my friends are sitting.

I roll my eyes. "Yeah, you've been replaced. He's my best friend now."

"Rude."

Beside me, Tera laughs. Tera's the first friend I made

freshman year from outside my own town. It's a weird thing about transitioning to high school. You don't think your childhood friendships will fade, but really Sky is the only grade-school friend I'm still close with. Tera lives in St. Elm, and she sat next to me in computer science my first day. I don't remember exactly what we talked about, but I do remember knowing after I'd left the class that I'd just made a friend.

"He asked about you when you were gone, you know." Tera's boyfriend, Roman, leans back in his chair to look at me past Tera's white-blond head. Roman was enveloped into our friendship group when he started dating Tera last spring. He's been friends with Liam for a long time because they both went to school and played sports in Hen Falls, though they weren't in the same grade. Roman's a junior like us. I always figured maybe it was a case of beautiful people sticking together. Roman has gray eyes, brown skin, and dimpled cheeks. His mom's white and his dad's Mexican, and they're both unreasonably attractive.

"He was probably hoping I would stay in the hospital long enough that Hunter would have to quit the soccer team and he could be the lone star," I say ungenerously.

"Amelia." Roman's tone is reproachful. "I think he . . ." He stops, running a hand over his closely shorn hair. "Let's just say I think he was genuinely relieved when you were okay, and leave it at that."

"Whaaaat." Sky is glowing with glee about this new piece of gossip. "You can*not* leave it at that. Is he into her? Amelia, would *you* be interested?"

"I think we should talk about something else."

It has not escaped my notice that the fifth member of our table, Grace, has been completely silent. She sits next to Skylar, drawing patterns in her ketchup with a french fry. Grace is a dorm student; she lives in Manhattan with wealthy parents and started going here last year. She has bushy hair, brown eyes, and dark skin. She has taught me everything I know about makeup, because she's the only one of my friends who was patient enough to keep explaining until it finally clicked. Every time I look at her, I get a fluttering, confused feeling in the pit of my stomach.

And about a week before my accident, I made a complete idiot of myself with her, and we haven't quite recovered from the awkwardness. Or I haven't, anyway. So now I'm reading into everything she says or doesn't say, and it hurts my brain. More than the concussion.

"Liam's kind of nice, you know," says Tera, not helping.

"And my brother would definitely murder me. Or him, more likely," I remind her. Even though I can't help but glance over to where Liam's sitting with some of his teammates. Despite how much I'm brushing off all this teasing, it does actually bother me, what he said. That it's my fault we're not friends. I've always steered clear because of Hunter, but Liam hasn't exactly come begging for my friendship, either.

"Have you added any new insects to your collection?" Grace asks. Then, in response to what I can only assume is a startled expression on my face, she laughs and says, "You asked for a subject change. You're welcome."

"I haven't," I answer. "I've been a little . . . I've just been busy."

It's a weak excuse, but I don't want to say I'm preoccupied because I don't want to talk about what's occupying me. My fears that someone tried to murder me, my broken wrist, my doctor's appointments, the lingering effects of my concussion. The more I'm fussed over, the worse I feel.

"What am I supposed to do if you don't find new crawling things to creep me out when I spend the night at your house?" Sky asks.

I laugh. "If you insist, I'll hunt down a barn spider this weekend."

Her full-body shudder is the perfect response. This is how we are, usually. Just ourselves. Friends who love each other despite very different interests. It's what I need to find my way back to, because it's not how things have been ever since I got home from the hospital. And it isn't everyone else who's being weird—not anymore.

It's *me*.

3

Soccer practice was rained out, but the school seems to think that if the boys go one day without exercise, they'll suddenly all be unable to kick a ball, so their coach has them run laps around the basketball court until the football team is done with the weight room, and then they move in on the weight machines.

Since Hunter drives Sky and me home—unless we want to take the bus, which we do *not*—we are sitting in the hallway of the athletic building doing homework. Across from the mostly glass wall of the weight room, of course, because we are only human, after all.

"Math is stupid," says Sky, massaging her temples. "Who even needs it?"

"Everyone," I say dryly. "And just FYI there's a spider approaching."

Sky glances to her left and then practically lunges across me to escape. Laughing, I set down my math homework and scoop up the delicate cellar spider that's casually traveling along the edge of the wall. I am actually a complete weirdo about bugs. I like to free them outside when I can, just because it feels like it should be nature that kills them, not me. I have no illusions about their short and brutal life cycles; I just like looking at them, watching the way they move. I don't have whatever it is that makes people recoil from the thought of touching any kind of bug. I used to be teased about it when I was younger, but I've improved at choosing my friends as I've gotten older, I guess.

It's still pouring outside, but there are eaves over one of the back entrances to the athletic building, so that's where I go, spider cupped in a loose fist. I set it down on the side of the walkway and silently wish it good luck.

When I go back inside, Liam is standing there. Of course.

"Did I just see you free a spider?" he asks, looking mildly horrified.

"You most certainly did. But aren't you supposed to be lifting weights right now?"

"I had to see the physical therapist," he says, nodding his head in the direction of the PT's office. "Twisted my ankle a few weeks ago, and it's still not quite right."

"Oh."

We're both going the same direction, but walking down the hallway beside him is awkward. I feel like I need to say something else, but I don't want to ask about his twisted ankle and open the door for him to ask about *my* injuries. Especially because I can see him eyeing my cast.

"So why, exactly, did you not just kill it?" he asks, breaking a tense silence.

I shrug. "Feels less gross to let the thing go outside than to smear its guts on the wall."

"Fair enough." His eyes dart to my spider-carrying hand.

"Are you afraid of spider germs?" I ask. I flex my fingers in his general direction, and he shies away. "Oh my God, you know spiders don't really have germs, right?"

"I know," he says coolly. "I just don't like dirt that much."

"Okay, well, can I explain something to you about a soccer field?"

He laughs at that, which is of course the exact moment we round the corner. Halfway down the hall, Sky looks up from her homework and then quickly and unsubtly back down at it.

"You know, this is a much better conversation than the one we had earlier," he says.

"Is it? All I've done is threaten to smear spider guts on you." Talking to Liam is giving me that fluttery feeling in my gut, and I wish I could request the fluttery feeling to just once choose a target with less disaster potential.

"Yeah, but you *didn't* smear spider guts on me, so that's something."

"Wow. I set the bar so low."

"I get it," he says, his tone suddenly serious. "But I do want you to know that I meant it, earlier, when I said it was good to see you back."

And then he pushes open the door to the weight room, and he's gone.

I feel weird and flushed and confused, but I sit down next

to Sky like everything is the same as it was when I left her five minutes ago. She doesn't say a thing, and she doesn't even glance my way, but she's got a big smirk on her face.

"Something amusing on your math homework?" I ask.

"Yeah, it's just this one problem about how big of an area will be hit by the nuclear meltdown when you inevitably start dating him and your brother finds out."

"Hilarious."

"Oh, come on." She squeezes my arm. "You know I'm just teasing. But he *is* hot, and you've run into him twice in one day. It almost feels like fate."

"Twice in one day at the school we both go to," I say dryly. "It's like a rom-com."

Still, I can't deny that our interactions today were unusual. It's not like I *never* spoke to him before. He doesn't socialize with the other soccer guys all that much outside of school and sports, but he's always . . . *around*. There have been times when we were forced to make small talk, but it's only ever been that—small.

There is a part of me, though, that's always felt bad for Liam. His mom left when he was a little kid, and there were a lot of rumors surrounding her departure. Before she left, the police were at their house all the time. People still talk about it. His parents were people who tried to act like everything was normal in public but had such big fights at home that the neighbors a quarter mile away got worried. His dad is grouchy and mean, which made it easy for people to believe all sorts of things—the most popular theory being that it's all a big lie and she's dead and buried somewhere on his vast property. Liam's dad has done nothing to quell the rumors, either. He continues to be creepy, and he comes to fewer and fewer of Liam's school and sports activities as time goes on. I'd like to believe if something awful was going on at home, Liam would have been taken away long ago, but I know sometimes it doesn't work out that way. The rumors are rough, regardless, and I think his life has been pretty hard.

I glance into the weight room, where Liam is wiping sweat off his face with the bottom of his shirt. I sigh. "How big *do* you think the nuclear blast radius would be?"

4

Doctor's appointments are getting really old. Hunter drops me off at the St. Elm hospital, so in addition to yet another checkup I will also experience the joy of riding a bus from here to school afterward. The bus is always filled mostly with elderly people, and it always smells terrible and never seems quite clean.

This isn't the hospital I went to after my accident, but it's where I've been visiting specialists, since it's more convenient to the academy. Even walking through its doors ties my shoulder muscles to my spine with tension. I hate the feel of the hospital, where you know terrible, stressful things are happening constantly, even though the halls you're walking through are mostly abandoned. The waiting room for my neurologist is dead silent, and when I accidentally drop my phone pulling it out of my pocket, I feel like I'm about to be scolded.

I told Grace yesterday that I'd be missing the first-period class we share, but she's sent me a text anyway: I can't believe you are abandoning me!!! 😱

It makes me smile. I text back: You know I'd rather be there than having my brain examined . . .

Glad you're making sure it's still in one piece, tho.

That takes the smile away. It's not her fault, but I want them all to stop saying things like this. I'm already too aware of my brain. Questioning it constantly. I left the hospital the first time with a big list of things to watch out for, and so far, it's done nothing except make me paranoid. I'm clutching a copy of that list now, in fact, the one Mom marked up last night after grilling me extensively to determine which symptoms I'm experiencing and which ones I'm not and which ones are new and which ones are old and what's bothering me the most and—

I realize I'm clenching the paper too tight in my hand, wrinkling it. I don't want to worry about this. Don't like thinking about my brain slamming against my skull and hiding secret wounds. All I want to think about is getting better, letting my wrist bones heal and my brain and ribs and bruised limbs rest. I don't want to be afraid. Of my brain, or of something happening to me again.

I'm still stewing when my neurologist calls me in. She's a nice lady with a warm smile and a soft voice.

My appointment's pretty quick; it's the third time I've seen her, and she seems to feel pretty good about how I'm doing. I wish that her confidence could inspire more of my own, but that's life I guess. She sends me off with a quickly scrawled note for my mom and a squeeze of my arm, and then it's time for my dreaded bus ride. I wait outside the hospital, shivering in my not-quite-warm-enough jacket.

"Amelia!"

I turn at the sound of my name. It's the guy who owns the house next to ours in Maple Hill, waving to me as he crosses the parking lot toward the building. He's in his early forties, same as my parents, and he moved in across the road from us a couple of years ago.

"Hi, Mr. Omerton," I say, clutching the straps of my backpack.

"Don't I always tell you to call me Calvin?" He smiles at me. "Mr. Omerton makes me sound so old, and I'm not old, am I?"

I don't know how to answer that, so I just laugh lightly. He does the same.

"Are you waiting for someone?" he asks.

I don't know why his question makes me uncomfortable, but it does. "I'm waiting for the bus. Heading back to school."

"You want a ride? Let me take you."

"No." I say it too fast. I smile brightly and try again: "It's nice of you to offer, but I wouldn't want you to be late for work. I'm happy to ride the bus."

"Don't be silly. No one's happy to ride the bus."

"Well, I am."

There's no reason for me to reject his offer. He's nice. Friendly. Comes over to chat sometimes when Dad's working in his shop. I haven't heard anyone in town say a single bad thing about him.

But lately, he creeps me out. My room faces the road, and a few times recently I've glanced out my window to the sight of his silhouette in one of his own windows. Looking directly back at me. I don't like it, and I don't want to be in a car alone with him.

"All right, all right." He chuckles. "I get it, having someone your parents' age drop you off at school isn't cool. Enjoy the bus, Amelia."

He lingers for a moment longer, and I think I'm supposed to change my mind, tell him no, it's not uncool, but I feel like he's trying to manipulate me, so I smile and say, "Thanks, I will. See you around."

The bus arrives a couple of minutes later. There are only a few other people on it right now, and one of them has a wet cough.

Still, I don't regret my decision at all.

It's just my luck that when I make it back to school and stop in the bathroom, Clarissa Everly walks in with one of her friends. I'd recognize her obnoxious laugh anywhere. Clarissa's a sophomore, and she dated my brother for a couple of months last year. They broke up right before summer vacation, and I know the real reason is that Hunter wasn't interested anymore, but whatever he said to let her down easy has given her the impression that she still has a chance to win him back. The thing is, though, she hates me. And the feeling's mutual.

The bathroom's big, and I'm all the way at the far end, so they don't notice my feet from where they stopped to touch up their makeup in the mirrors over the sinks. I'm planning to emerge and just ignore them, but the first thing Clarissa says is, "My mom thinks Maria Lugen didn't die by accident."

Everything inside me freezes.

"Really?" says the friend. "What else could have happened?"

"Suicide."

I unfreeze, and my stomach plummets to my feet. I've been so wrapped up in the similarities between what happened to me and to her, I hadn't even considered other possible ways in which her accident might not have been an accident. I don't know a thing about Maria Lugen. I'd never even heard of her until she went missing, a couple of weeks before my accident.

"What did she even have to be unhappy about?" asks the friend, who clearly doesn't understand how depression works.

"I don't know," says Clarissa. I can't see them, but I can hear the shrug in her voice. "But what did Amelia Stern have to be unhappy about, either, and *she* tried to kill herself. Who knows why people do these things."

Now my stomach has removed itself from my body altogether. This topic did, of course, come up when I was in the hospital, along with the six million other questions I was asked, but—maybe foolishly—I haven't thought about it since. Is that what people think? Hearing Clarissa say it is one thing, but now I can't help wondering who else believes this. My parents? Friends? Brother? It makes me furious that she thinks it's okay to casually speculate about my mental health, like someone trying to commit suicide is all a big joke. Maybe she never got close enough to Hunter to know that it isn't *me* in our family who lives with depression. Maybe she wouldn't think it's so funny if she knew Hunter takes a pill every morning to help him keep those kinds of thoughts at bay.

I burst out of my stall, scowling, and they both stare, shocked. The friend looks ashamed, but Clarissa doesn't.

"Hi, Amelia," she says.

"I wasn't trying to kill myself," I answer, aggressively turning on the sink. "It was a freak accident. But even if I *was*, do you think it's something hilarious for you to gossip about in a bathroom? And Maria isn't here to defend herself. She's *gone*, and her family has to mourn her. You don't think they have enough to worry about without people spreading rumors?"

Clarissa still doesn't look ashamed, so as I rip a piece of paper towel to dry my hands I add, "I'll be sure to tell Hunter I ran into you today. See you around."

"Amelia, wait—"

I slam the bathroom door in her face.

5

I'm still stewing about what Clarissa said when Hunter and I get home from school. Mom's nearly done cooking dinner; Aunt Jenna is in the kitchen with her, and they've each got a glass of wine. Here's the thing about Maple Hill: People who grow up here don't seem to leave. Or if they do leave, something pulls them back. Mom and Aunt Jenna are no exception—they both went away for college and both convinced their husbands that *this* was the place where they should spend the rest of their lives. Aunt Jenna is a physical therapist at the hospital in Forestville. Uncle Cliff works at the local chicken farm, the only business that anyone outside this area's ever heard of. I work there part-time in the summer, packing eggs.

Sometimes I think that when I'm older, I'd like to live in a city. Grace talks about Manhattan so lovingly, it makes me want to see what it'd be like to live in a world so completely opposite to mine. But part of me also can't picture living anywhere else. There's a reason people come back, a reason they put up with spotty cell service and a town with literally zero stores. With tiny populations and petty gossip. I know I'm only sixteen, but I *get* it. It's sort of an indefinable thing. A feeling of rightness in your heart. The sense that every ounce of love you feel for this place, it feels for you, too.

Hunter dumps his smelly gym bag next to the kitchen table, but Mom glares at it for two seconds and he sheepishly carries it up to his room.

"How was your appointment?" she asks me.

"Good, I think." I hand her the note from my doctor. She reads it and seems satisfied.

"And how was school?"

"Fine. A little boring. Finished all my homework while Hunter was at practice." I slide onto one of the stools at the kitchen peninsula, eyeing the smudged lipstick on the rim of Aunt Jenna's wine glass. I like that my mom still hangs out with her sister so often. I hope Hunter and I can be friends as adults, too, as dorky as that may be. "When's Dad getting home? Tomorrow?"

Mom pulls a lasagna out of the oven. "I can't remember. Let me text him."

"Great job keeping track of your husband's schedule," Aunt Jenna teases.

Mom laughs, her fingers busy tapping out a text message. "I'd like to see *you* try it." Her phone buzzes about five seconds later. "Yep, tomorrow. Probably while you're at school."

"Good. Maybe we can go hiking this weekend?"

"I'm sure Dad'll be up for it. Go tell your brother dinner's ready."

"Hunter! Dinner's ready!" I bellow in the direction of the stairs.

"Amelia. Did your feet stop working, or were you just hoping to blow my eardrums out of my body?" Mom's expression is less than amused.

I shrug unapologetically.

"Well, in case you worried about a lung injury," says Aunt Jenna.

Mom doesn't have much of a sense of humor about any of my injuries, but Aunt Jenna seems to be an exception. *I'm* not allowed to make jokes, but whatever.

"I am *not* the loudest person in our family," I say coolly as Hunter bounds down the stairs like an entire herd of elephants.

Aunt Jenna stays for dinner—Uncle Cliff and their son, Conner, who's eleven, are preparing to go hunting this weekend, and Aunt Jenna says she's trying to avoid getting sent to the store. It's probably a good call. Every year, they end up needing something, and they always send her to get it, and she always gets the wrong thing. But I was sort of hoping to catch Mom alone this evening and ask her if she thought I was trying to hurt myself when I fell. I don't want her to have even considered it, and if she did, I want to reassure her that I absolutely was not. But I don't want to talk about it in front of Aunt Jenna, and I *really* don't want to talk about it in front of Hunter, who would be furious to know what Clarissa had said. And hurt, too, probably.

So after we help Mom clean up, I wander to my room with

my phone for some good old-fashioned social media stalking. I feel weird looking at a dead girl's Facebook page, but I type Maria Lugen's name into the search anyway. She's the top result—her profile picture is of herself with a calf and a blue ribbon at the fair. I don't know much about her, but I know her family has a farm on the outskirts of St. Elm and that she and her brother always showed animals. We only have a few mutual friends and her page has good security, so I can't see much besides her profile pictures. Her smiling face stares back at me from each one, and I feel ill.

I find her brother, Steve, who's a freshman at the academy. His page isn't as secured, but he's a fourteen-year-old boy, so there's not a lot to see. Mostly it's condolences from friends and pictures of himself fishing or hunting. Some memes and jokes. I don't know what I expected. I just wanted to know something, *anything*, about Maria. Something that connects us. Doubt seeps into me. Maybe there really isn't more here, and I'm making something of my accident out of nothing. I wish I could settle one way or the other—it was an accident, or it wasn't—but I vacillate wildly instead. Sometimes I trust the instinct in my gut and other times I think my brain's playing tricks on me.

Discouraged, I try Instagram. But it's no help, either. More pictures of her, alone and with friends, laughing and happy. Pictures of the sunset from her incredibly beautiful house. Flowers. Scenery. Typical stuff. The captions don't offer much insight. She's a "describe this picture exactly" kind of girl, not a "make an analogy about the fleeting glory of life" person.

With a sigh, I back out of her profile to my feed. At the top is a picture of Grace standing in front of the library at school, arms open like she's showing off its glass-and-brick facade. I double tap it, ignoring the way my stomach ties itself into a knot at the sight of her. My troll brain reminds me of what happened weeks ago, how much I messed up our friendship with my awkwardness, and my cheeks burn with shame.

A week before my accident, Grace and I were working on homework together in the library while I waited for Hunter's practice to end. It was practically empty and we sat on one of the big, cushy leather couches in front of the faux fireplace in the lounge area. And I decided it was time to ask her advice about something I wasn't sure I was really all that ready to talk about yet.

"Hey, Grace," I asked, setting my biology textbook on the arm of the couch. "Can I ask you a weird and personal question?"

She set down her homework and turned toward me with a smile. "Uh, obviously. Always."

"How did you know you were a lesbian?" It came out a lot blunter than I'd meant for it to.

"Oh. Well. That was . . . okay, that was not what I expected at all." She straightened her ponytail and looked me directly in the eye. I had to command myself not to look away. It was me who'd asked, after all. "So I guess I . . . I don't know. I just knew? I could tell when a guy was attractive because, well, we all know what makes someone appealing. But I didn't want to do anything about it, I guess. I thought, 'Okay, that's a nice-looking person, good for him.' But girls, I thought about. When I saw an attractive girl, I kind of like, felt it inside me, you know? I was interested. I guess that's how I figured it out. It wasn't a lightbulb moment or anything. Maybe it's different for other people. But that's how it worked for me. Why . . . um, why are you asking?"

I broke eye contact then. "Well, I'm definitely attracted to boys, but I sort of think . . . maybe not just boys. But I don't know how I . . . How do I know? What if I'm . . . I don't know. I feel confused, and I don't know what to say or how to explain."

She smiled. "I understand. I mean, it *is* confusing. But you can just . . . You can let yourself figure it out, you know? You don't have to put a label on how you're feeling unless you want to."

"That's true." I stared down at my fingernails. What I didn't tell her was that it was *her* who made me the most confused. That it'd started sometime last spring and had only gotten worse while she was home for the summer, when all I saw of her was from her Instagram feed, which was mostly bikini-clad selfies. That feeling this way about her made me look back on so many other things through a totally different lens. All the times I thought I was admiring girls because I wanted to be like them, when actually it was that I wanted to be *with* them.

"I wish I had better advice," she said. "I don't think I was very helpful."

"No, you were. I—" My Fitbit beeped then, a text from

Hunter to meet him in the athletic building in five minutes. I sighed. "Guess it's time for me to head home."

"Okay." She looked sort of worried, like maybe I made it up to get away from her. We packed our things in silence, but when we were done, she looked at me, biting her lip anxiously.

"Thank you," I told her, because I didn't know what else to say. "This probably won't be the last you hear from me about this. It felt . . . kind of good to say something."

"Good, I'm glad." She hugged me tight.

I had that fluttery feeling again, the same one as when I get a crush on a boy. And the fluttery feeling turns me into a true idiot.

"It's, um—you're what made me wonder," I blurted as soon as the hug was over.

She looked at me oddly, an expression I couldn't parse. "You mean, like, because . . ."

I wanted to shrivel up and die on the spot. "Forget I said that. I just—I have to go."

She called after me, but I straight up fled.

I didn't want to hear her let me down, no matter how gently she did it. I didn't want her to *know* in the first place. She lives in New York. She has a billion choices better than me. So I simply removed myself from the situation, and I haven't been alone with her since.

Thinking about that incident makes me die inside all over again, and I need a distraction *badly*. Before I can think about it, I find myself searching for Liam. His Instagram is private, because of course it is. He and I don't follow each other on social media at all, per the unspoken loyalty pledge I apparently made to my brother at birth. But I think about what he said the other day in the cafeteria. Whose fault is it that we're not friends? Before I can talk myself out of it, I hit the follow request button and then throw the phone away from myself.

I'm cleaning my glasses with my shirt and trying to figure out what to do with all my restlessness when my phone trills with a notification. Heart racing, I snatch it up.

It's a text from my brother. Science is stupid. Come help me.

A follow-up text comes while I'm busy rolling my eyes at the first one: Please.

I sigh and cross the hall to his room, phone in hand. "You know if you had taken anatomy like I told you to, you'd be finding sports medicine super easy."

"I doubt it." He shoves his textbook toward me, open to a page with the muscles of the human body all labeled. "Why are all the names so similar? How am I supposed to remember where they are?"

"Flash cards," I answer. I set down my phone on his desk and pick up a stack of index cards that have probably been sitting there since the beginning of the school year. There's dust on top of them. "Just keep cycling through them until you remember them all." I start scribbling info on the first card and add, "It helps if you shut off Fortnite while you're studying, by the way."

I expected a laugh or a snide response out of that, so when

nothing comes, I look up. Hunter's frowning at my phone, which is lit up with a notification. A pit of foreboding lodges in my stomach.

"Liam Hawthorne has accepted your follow request," he says aloud.

I swipe my phone off his desk, which is fortunate because he misses the next notification: *Liam Hawthorne followed you back.*

"Why are you following Liam on Instagram all of a sudden?" Hunter demands.

"Because I want to," I say coolly, still scribbling on his notecards. "He's talked to me a couple of times recently, and I just kinda thought . . . why can't we be friendly?"

"Because he's Satan, that's why."

I scoff. "Hunter. Come on. You know he's not *that* bad. And he's friends with Roman, so, I don't know. It's not like I announced that we're getting married next week or something."

Hunter turns back to his computer and quits Fortnite. That's not a good sign. "Do you mean that you're thinking about dating him? Is that what's happening?"

"Not really. I barely know him. But I need something to think about other than . . . other than my head and that murdered girl and—"

"Murdered girl?" he interrupts. "What are you talking about?"

"Oh, uh . . . that girl who drowned in the Passumpsic. I thought it seemed . . . It seems similar to what happened to me, is all."

Hunter picks up a pen and taps it against his desk. I wait,

patient and quiet, while he mulls. "You think someone tried to murder you? Who would do that?"

I shrug. "Don't know. All I know is, I've sat on that guard-rail a billion times and I've never gotten too close to the edge of that hill, and I've *definitely* never been careless while I was sitting there. And I know the doctors said it was my imagination, but I *swear* I felt someone . . . I don't know, *pushing* me, I guess, right before I stopped remembering anything. So I just . . . Don't worry about it, okay? Everything's felt kinda weird since that happened to me. That's all."

"Who else have you talked to about this? Sky?"

I shake my head. "No, not Sky. Or anyone. I know it sounds a little crazy, and I don't really need people thinking I'm, like, delusional or something."

"I hadn't thought about it," he says, brow furrowed. "I guess . . . I mean, it *is* sort of an odd coincidence."

He looks disturbed, and I feel bad that I even brought this up. "It probably *is* a coincidence. Please don't worry about it. Maybe I just don't want to be the girl who tripped and almost died, I don't know."

"Yeah, probably. Just . . . be careful, all right?"

I stand up and hand him the finished index cards. "Here you go. Science is easy when you have index cards."

I smile as I leave, but it's strained. I wish he'd just told me I was being ridiculous.

6

I decide to use my free period the next day to research, but the problem is, I have no idea what I'm researching. I'm not an investigator and I have no clues.

I sit at one of the long tables in the library and open a notebook to a blank page. The longer I stare at the page, the blanker it seems. Like the blue stripes are taunting me. Like they know I have nowhere to begin.

People who hate me

I scrawl it at the top of the page, think for a moment, then cross it out.

People I'm suspicious of

That feels better, but who am I suspicious of?

Sky, I think. I hate that her name comes to mind first, but why won't she tell me what her big important secret was? And why don't I feel like I can tell her my fears? I don't know why I have such an untrusting nature; nothing's happened in my life to make me this way, but I always suspect that people have ulterior motives or secret second lives. My imagination is too wild.

Skylar Stewart
Mr. Omerton
Steve Lugen (or someone else in that
family...?)
Clarissa Reed

That last one is just me being petty. But Sky, my creepy neighbor, and someone in Maria Lugen's family . . . that's my whole pathetic list. I frown down at the page. It's too short. There are definitely more suspicious people than this in my life. I scratch absently at an itch on my palm, just inside my cast. No other names come to me.

I flip to the next page and write:

To-Do List:
1. Add more suspicious people
2. Start ruling out some of them
3. Get better at this

"What're you doing?"

Liam's voice at my shoulder startles me entirely out of my skin. I cover the embarrassing to-do list with my palm.

"What am *I* doing? Not sneaking up on girls in the library like a creep show."

He grins and pulls a chair up beside me. I shift in mine—they're the uncomfortable kind, fake wood with a little ridge in the center as though my butt cheeks need to be kept separated.

"You have free period now, too?" he asks.

"Tuesday and Thursday, yeah."

"Okay, well, I wasn't *trying* to be a creep, but that is one weird to-do list."

I grimace and remove my hand from the notebook. At least he didn't see my pathetic list of suspicious people. "Yeah, I don't think I know you well enough to explain this."

He tilts his head, rests his forearm on the table. "Try me."

He nudges my notebook with a finger until its edge is parallel to the table's edge. This level of neurosis should probably be a turnoff, but I think it's having the opposite effect on me. As it turns out, the giant barrier I kept between Liam and me all these years is all that kept me from being completely won over by his charms. And by charms, I mean his incredibly handsome face and compelling smile and intense attention to detail. I resist the urge to shut the notebook. He's already seen the to-do list; it doesn't matter now.

I take a breath and start with what I think is a reasonable question. "How many accidents where people drowned after falling into the river—sober—can you remember in your whole lifetime?"

"Uh, well . . ." He looks at me like he's putting it all together, and I kind of regret saying anything. I'm trusting Liam Hawthorne of all people with my deepest fears? I'm barely okay with having told Hunter.

"Listen, I know this is probably dumb. That's why I'm making my weird list alone in the library. It's just something I can't quite . . . I can't wonder about it and do nothing, so I've gotta do something."

He nods like this all makes perfect sense. "I'll help you, if you want."

"Why would you do that?"

"Because you don't think a whole lot of me." He holds up a finger when I start to protest, then leans in closer and hypnotizes me with those blue, blue eyes. "And I plan on doing whatever it takes to change your mind."

I don't know what to say, so I scratch my palm again and say nothing.

"Does that hurt?" He gestures to my wrist.

"Not really. Mostly it just itches."

"How's the rest of you?"

I narrow my eyes. "You mean how's my head, right?"

"I see that I've touched a nerve. But no, I wasn't asking specifically about your head. You must have more injuries than your head and your wrist."

"I had a lot of bruises, but they're all pretty much gone now. My ribs are still a little sore, and my left kneecap for some reason. My head is . . . It's fine."

"I'm sorry about your left kneecap. And whatever it is in your head that's still bothering you."

I reach for the necklace that isn't there. I guess I'm never going to break that nervous habit. "It's only occasional headaches. A little vertigo. Common post-concussion stuff. But I don't like having that little missing piece of memory."

"That's pretty common, too, though, isn't it?" He leans closer to me, and I can smell his cologne. Not too strong; the perfect amount. "That you don't remember the time surrounding a concussion?"

"Yeah." I frown at the table. "But just because something's common doesn't mean it's fun."

"You really don't remember it? At all?"

I shake my head. "And I'm told I never will."

"Huh." He looks pensive.

"I know. It's a regular soap opera over here."

He laughs, and it makes me feel like I'm experiencing a memory.

"I think someone was laughing," I blurt out. He looks baffled, so I elaborate. "When I was, um, had my accident. When you laughed, I had the strongest feeling that I remembered laughter while I was falling."

His eyebrows lift, surprised. "Like, a man laughing?"

I shrug. "I don't know what it sounded like, I just think . . . it was there."

"So you *can* remember things, then. It's coming back to

you." There's an intensity to his gaze that sends a thrill down my spine. "Maybe you'll remember everything after all."

"I don't think so. The doctors seemed confident that I wouldn't, and I've tried everything I could think of to trigger something more. The laughter was probably something I already remembered, and I didn't realize it. Another sensory thing, like being pushed or the feeling when my necklace broke free. Or it could be nothing. When I mentioned those things to my nurse at the hospital, she seemed to think that I should tell my doctor, but he was kind of . . . He said that it can be really confusing when you're trying to recall a memory that isn't there and that I'm probably projecting. I think I explained that badly, but I . . . Well, you don't want to hear all this."

"Yes, I do." He leans toward me again, and I'm uncomfortable with how not-uncomfortable his nearness feels.

"Why?" The question comes out as a whisper. I should stop asking him that, but I don't understand why he even cares.

"Because if I'm going to help you, as I told you already that I will, I've gotta know everything. Besides, no one ever got bored listening to someone talk about something this wild."

I smile, pushing my glasses higher on my nose. "You think I can't make this boring?"

He leans back in his seat and returns my smile, only his is smoldering. "I'd like to see you try."

As my friends and I head down to the soccer field for a game a couple of days later, I find myself thinking about Liam. It's a

46

welcome change, to be honest, from my recent Grace fixation. Even with the whole Hunter complication, it's simpler to be interested in Liam. I've dated boys before, and the familiarity of having a crush on a boy is feeling pretty good with everything else uncertain in my life right now.

My justice notebook sits among all the others in my backpack, outwardly unremarkable. But its pages aren't so aggressively blank as they were yesterday.

Liam helped a lot—and by that I mean he completely took over. He told me creating a numbered to-do list wasn't helpful unless there were actual linear steps. That I should create action items with checkboxes so I can feel accomplished.

He's actually kind of a major dorky weirdo, and I'm into it. Which I hate. Hunter would loathe how much time we've spent together already. Maybe I shouldn't care so much what my brother thinks about who I'm interested in, and usually I don't. But Liam and Hunter have a history that long predates me even knowing Liam existed. Hunter's dislike of Liam is kind of his one high-maintenance thing, so I've always respected it. But *should* I? Liam seems interested in me all of a sudden, and while that triggers questions from the suspicious side of me, it's also . . . Well, it's always nice to be wanted.

It's a perfect day for watching soccer. The sky overhead is pure blue, its edges lined with splashes of stray clouds like spilled milk. And according to Hunter, the team we're playing isn't very good, so it should be an easy win. The whole environment is so relaxed compared to normal. It's like all the fans know this won't be close and they don't need to be tense. I've been fighting a losing battle against a headache all day, but I'm hoping that pretending it doesn't exist will eventually make it go away.

"Who wants to bet with me on who will score the most goals?" Grace asks. "Ten bucks says Hunter."

"I'm so not stepping into that minefield," I say. She's probably right about Hunter; he's played well lately, and Liam's been a little off this season. My theory is that his twisted ankle is still bothering him, even though the only time he's mentioned it was that one day when I saw him in the hallway of the athletic building.

"Me neither," says Roman.

"I'll do ten on Liam, if you all *swear* not to tell Hunter." Sky digs in her pocket, retrieving some crumpled bills.

"Betrayal!" I fake gasp, and she shoves me. She may not be his sister, but Hunter would be just as mad to learn that she bet against him as he would if I'd done it.

"I never make gambles I'm not sure about," Tera says.

"Yeah, when I think risk-taker, you're the last person I think of," Grace says sarcastically.

"With *money*." Tera sticks out her tongue. "But fine, I've only got eight dollars, but I'll put it on Liam."

Grace takes her money gleefully. "I better win. There's this new eyeliner I've been wanting to try, but it costs, like, thirty dollars."

"Thirty dollars?" Roman asks incredulously. "What is it, made of gold?"

"Platinum." Grace laughs. "Hey—there goes Hunter. I'm one up!"

"I'm already regretting my choices," Sky mutters.

While my friends watch the game, deeply invested in their bet, I watch the stands. Soccer games at St. Elm used to be sparsely attended events. There wasn't much to see, and it's not as popular a fall sport here as football is. But Hunter and Liam have made it fun to watch. It isn't only that they're talented—which they both very much are—but the way they've led the team. Even as freshmen, they were leaders. Their personal rivalry has never been a factor on the field. They set it all aside and work together seamlessly to keep their team on track. And they've attracted an audience for the games that goes beyond just family members.

As I look across the faces of all those enthusiastic soccer fans, I can't help but think about how little we ever really know about the people around us. The strangers, I mean. Unless there are obvious signs, you don't know anything about what they're really like. The guy screaming at the ref might go home and be the best dad in the world. The one sitting quietly and clapping politely for both teams could be a murderer.

We like to think if we do everything right and don't make dumb choices, we'll be safe, but the reality is that anyone could be thinking about hurting you at any time and you may never even know it.

The person who tried to kill me could be in these stands right now. I shudder thinking about it.

Liam scores a goal, and Sky cheers way too loudly next to my ear.

"Careful," I tell her, "or Hunter might banish you from our car."

She hooks her arm around mine. "You would never let him do that."

I smirk. "Or would I?"

Grace leans forward from behind us, resting her chin on both our shoulders. The smell of her perfume ties my stomach in a knot. Her hand grazes my lower back, and I don't know if it's on purpose or not, but I really hope not because otherwise it seems almost cruel, knowing what she knows about how I feel. Or maybe she's just trying to maintain normalcy. It's so hard to tell.

"I know you said you were staying out of it," she says, "but who would you have bet on?"

"Hunter," I say easily, though I'm not sure it's true. "But I wouldn't want you to have to split your winnings. You should get that eyeliner."

She grins broadly, which tightens the knot in my stomach. I want to tell her I changed my mind, that I would actually bet on Liam, but I'd only be saying it out of spite, and I try to reserve spite for people who really deserve it. Looking for signs that Grace might be jealous of Liam is not a good reason.

The game isn't close, and neither is the bet. Hunter scores double the amount of goals Liam does.

And when it's over, Sky and I start across the field to meet

Hunter, like usual, but I see Liam and accidentally-on-purpose get separated from Sky in a crowd of players and family members so I can head in his direction. Because that's who I've become, I guess.

"Great job today," I tell him.

He shrugs. "Hunter played better."

"Scoring more goals doesn't necessarily mean someone played better."

He gives me a flat look.

"Oh come on, Liam. You don't need to be this hard on yourself. It wasn't a challenging game for either one of you, so it's not like you had to pull out your best performances."

That elicits a small smile from him, finally. "Yeah, I guess I don't get as much satisfaction from easy victories."

"Personally, I like to take satisfaction from all levels of victory. It's really just an opportunity to brag about how great you are; you don't need to mention the part about how unworthy your opponent was."

"You're so wise." He smiles at me again, but then his gaze is drawn elsewhere. I follow it and see him watching my brother. Hunter's surrounded by my parents and Sky and Sky's parents and a few other people from Maple Hill who came just to watch him play. Liam's dad used to come to his games sometimes when he was a freshman, but I don't think I've even *seen* his father since Liam got a driver's license. Aside from whatever went on between Liam's parents before his mom left the picture, it's never been a secret that Liam's dad didn't want kids and that he remains bitter about the responsibility. That's not something I should know, probably, but it's something I've overheard my parents gossiping about before with their friends. Parents sometimes forget that we have ears, I think. I make a mental note to add Liam's dad to my list of suspicious people for no reason other than that he gives me a bad vibe.

"We always go for ice cream after games if it's not freezing out," I tell Liam. "You wanna join us?"

The flat look returns. "That's a nice offer, but I think I'll pass."

"But you just—"

"I'll see you Monday, okay?" he interrupts quickly, gives me a much more forced smile, and walks away.

I feel bad as I turn to join my family. Bad because I don't know why Liam rejected my offer—was it Hunter, or have I been misreading all his signals?—and bad because it doesn't seem fair that Liam has just as much talent as Hunter but no one to care about it.

And, I realize, I might want to be his person who cares. I don't feel bad about that, though. Not at all.

7

I'm in the woods near my house looking for insects when Tera texts me Saturday morning.

Grace and I are at Roman's. Come over!!!

I hesitate for a fraction of a second, because I texted Sky earlier, but she hasn't replied yet, so what the heck. Besides, I can hunt down backyard insects anytime.

On my way!

Roman's house is across the river. Hen Falls is in Vermont, but he's actually less than two miles from my house, unlike school, which is a twenty-minute drive.

I like to say I'm not athletic, but when Hunter was a freshman and I was an eighth grader, he convinced me to start going for runs with him in the early morning when he said it was too creepy to go alone. I grumbled at first. A *lot*. But now I kind of love it.

So I change into capri leggings, a tank top, and a light zip-up jacket that fits over my cast without much trouble. Then I grab my headphones, text Mom where I'm going, and set off.

My entomology podcast drowns out any noise around me, and I'm able to completely ignore the enthusiastic wave of greeting from Mr. Omerton. He's standing on his porch, watching me leave, but I pretend to be too immersed in my run to notice. Eventually, I'll need to talk to him if I'm going to eliminate him from my list. Or, you know, *not* eliminate him. But I'm not remotely up for it today.

My doctor cleared me for exercise last week, but running . . . hurts. I was mostly joking with Liam about my left kneecap, but running amplifies the pain of the injury. My whole body got so jostled by my fall that it's not enjoying this activity whatsoever. I grit my teeth and power on, but when I pass by the grade school, I slow to a walk, feeling dizzy and frustrated. My head clears as I reach the library, and I pick up my pace again. Turn left at the town hall and start toward the bridge leading into Hen Falls. The Hen Falls Reservoir is to the left of the bridge. It's much smaller than the Comerford Dam, and I'm not next to any steep embankment, but still my heart races as I approach.

Water isn't what hurt you, I remind myself.

But it killed Maria Lugen, my brain argues back. *And if that tree hadn't caught you, you'd have drowned just like she did.*

The river has become a Thing for me. Every day when Hunter drives us across the bridge to school, I hold my breath. My imagination goes wild with visions of my lungs filling up with water. I escaped death so narrowly, and I'm afraid the universe won't let it stand. That I was meant to die by water and, eventually, I will.

I look at the road behind me and the road across the bridge, and I avoid the pedestrian walkway that lines one edge, opting to run down the middle of the road instead. A car approaches from behind me just as I reach the Vermont side of the bridge and swerve casually back to the edge of the road like I've been there this whole time. It's stupid, really, because I could die getting hit by a car as easily as drowning in the river.

I'm still anxious when I reach Roman's a few minutes later, and I'm relieved that my friends aren't outside so I have a minute to catch my breath. I had to start walking again shortly after the bridge. Jogging is too much for me apparently. Another thing I can't do because my stupid body won't *heal* already. I wipe my glasses clean on my jacket, pacing in a slow circle until I feel like myself again.

Roman's apartment is in a big, beautiful house. It's common here. We have so many of these huge old homes that lend themselves perfectly to being segmented into apartments. This house has four, and Roman's is at the back of the house, farthest from the road. His mom is sitting in the living room when I walk in. She's reading a book with some pretty serious abs on the cover.

"Hi, Amelia." She smiles at me. "They're up there."

She gestures toward Roman's room. It's up a steep set of ladder-like stairs that enters a massive closet (which we all agree is wasted on Roman). His bedroom is beyond that, and his door is open. They're all three sitting on the floor in front of his bed. Grace is heckling while Roman and Tera play Mario Kart. I know better than to distract either of my fiercely competitive friends from the game, so I slip in quietly and sit next to Grace. My rib twinges.

"Tell me you didn't jog here," she says, plucking at the end of my pant leg.

"It's not that far. Hunter has the car. I think he's at some soccer thing."

"Nope," says Roman, not glancing away from his game for even a second. "I texted Liam earlier, and he's coming over in a bit."

"Oh. Well, I wasn't really listening when Hunter told me what he was doing." This is a complete lie. I'm *positive* he told me he was going to school for a mandatory soccer workout.

I'd like to say it was most likely Liam skipped it, but like Hunter, he would never. So . . . why is my brother lying to me?

"Liam's never hung out with us before. Why all of a sudden?"

I can feel Roman rolling his eyes at me, even looking at the back of his head. "I think you know why."

I adjust my glasses, wishing I hadn't asked. Grace stretches and leans her back against the side of the bed, which puts space between us.

"So you're feeling okay enough to jog again?" she asks. She's too observant.

"I walked some of the time. It wasn't bad."

Tera defeats Roman with a loud shriek of victory that nearly startles me out of my skin.

"Well, *that* was unnecessary," says Grace dryly. I'm grateful Tera distracted her. "Does this mean we can go outside now?"

I can tell Roman is stewing in his loss and dying for a rematch, but Tera kisses his cheek and says, "Yeah, absolutely."

We grab a bag of potato chips and some soda from the kitchen on our way out. The fall air is crisp and cool in my lungs. October is beautiful in New England, with the riot of color on the trees and temperatures that are cool but still bearable without wearing a ton of layers. We rake leaves from the lawn into a huge pile and take turns jumping into it. Well, I avoid the jumping part. No one presses the issue, and I'm relieved. I'm still frustrated that jogging was too much, and I don't want any more questions about my head or any other part of me.

When everyone's sufficiently coated in crumbling leaves and detritus, we cram together in the porch swing that hangs from a thick tree branch and pass the bag of chips back and forth. I'm sandwiched between Tera and Grace. Grace's arm rests half on my leg because there's really nowhere else to put it. She doesn't seem to mind my nearness, which bothers me, and I'm not sure why. It's not her fault I developed a crush on her, and I *want* our friendship to get back to normal, but.

Nothing's satisfying me lately. Everything has felt different since my accident, and I just want it to be like it was before. I want to be regular, and I don't want to be afraid. My world used to be so small and safe. And I'm happy to be learning and growing, to figure out more about who I am and who I want to be, but I just feel so *restless*. So itchy to get through the awkward phase where I confess crushes to people who don't like me back and on to the confident phase where I know exactly how to get what I want. And on to feeling safe enough to go after it.

As if on cue, Liam arrives.

His house is less than a mile up the road, and he rode his bike here. He leans it carefully against a tree and does that thing where he wipes his face with his shirt even though it doesn't look like he's sweating. It's fine. I'm not going to complain about a glimpse of his toned stomach.

"Just tell me," I say quickly to Roman, before Liam gets close enough to hear. "He likes me, right?"

Roman hesitates for a long moment. I think he's watching me watch Liam, feeling out what I'm going to do with the information. "Right."

Next to me, Grace shifts her weight. Her arm moves away from my leg. I don't know if it means something or if it means nothing, but I don't have to worry about that now, do I? I know Liam likes me, and I might as well admit that I'm not uninterested. It's all pretty simple. And simple is what I need.

"You're looking a little outnumbered," says Liam to Roman.

Roman grins. "Can't complain, though."

"Want a turn destroying our leaf pile?" I ask innocently, knowing full well that with Liam's feelings about dirt and germs, there's no way he'll jump into those leaves.

"Looks like you're all done," he says smoothly, narrowing his eyes at me. I smile so he knows I was teasing.

The five of us can't all fit on this swing, so we decide to go for a walk instead. Down by the river, at Tera's suggestion. I swallow the objections that push at my throat. It's good for me to go near the water, and to do it with a group of friends I trust. No one will hurt me. I repeat that to myself over and over as we cross the railroad tracks behind Roman's house and head down the hill. It's not that steep. No one is going to push me. I am going to be fine. I am fine.

Liam walks close to me, so close. Every time I sneak a glance at his face, he's got his eyes on my broken wrist. It makes me self-conscious. That cast should not be the most interesting thing about me.

After my fourth furtive glance, he catches me.

"When do you get that thing off?" he asks.

"Couple of weeks." I run my fingers over the bumpy surface. "Assuming it continues to heal right."

"Bizarre, isn't it?" he says. "How the human body can put itself back together like that?"

"I hadn't thought about it that much, but I guess it is." We've gotten kind of separated from the others, so I pick up my pace a little as we near the bottom of the slope. "I'm glad, though. Until they come up with robot bodies, we're stuck with what we've got, and I don't want what I've got to include a misshapen wrist."

"A robot body would definitely be preferred." Liam's pace is casual, like he doesn't really *want* to catch up with the others. "I'm getting out of this flesh suit the moment I can."

I laugh. "I bet robot bodies are expensive, so you'll have to save up. And we're falling behind; you'd better pick up the pace. I've seen you play soccer. I know you can move faster than this."

Liam's gaze flickers to the other three, who've stopped next to the river to wait for us. "I'm not sure they like me," he says.

"Oh come on. You've been friends with Roman forever."

"Not him, the girls."

"Don't be ridiculous. They barely know you. What's not to like?"

It's such an embarrassing thing to say, I can't look him in the eye any longer, and I hurry over to the others.

"About time," says Grace, hooking her arm around mine. "We thought we might have to send out a search party."

I laugh again and brave a glance at Liam, who smiles when I do.

"It's my fault," he says. "I kept distracting her."

We all move forward again, as a group, and Grace's arm slips free of mine as we do. I find myself, once again, walking next to Liam, but this time we're not so far behind.

"So . . . what are we doing for Halloween?" Grace asks. "*Please* tell me there's something to do. I've been preparing my costume for *months*."

"Has there *ever* been something to do?" Tera asks with a sigh. She's walking on the skinny trunk of a fallen tree, holding on to Roman's shoulder for balance.

Tera's not wrong. At our age, there aren't a lot of Halloween options. There are definitely parties, but not the kind I can go to if I want to keep my parents' trust, which I do. But this year . . . "Isn't one of the guys on the soccer team having a thing?" I glance to Liam for confirmation.

"Yeah, Alec. Well, his parents are having the party, technically." Liam shoves his hands in his pockets. "I wasn't planning to go, but . . . if you're all going, maybe I will."

"Aren't all your friends on the soccer team?" Grace asks. "Why wouldn't you go?"

Liam shrugs. "I'm not really that friendly with anyone on the team. And Alec, he's . . . We don't get along, that's all. I don't have to get along with everyone who plays soccer, do I?" All of us laugh, and he smiles sheepishly. "For the record, Hunter hates me way more than I hate him."

"Do you actually *hate* him?" I ask, because I can't help myself. Other than their former rivalry, Hunter can never cite a valid reason that the two of them don't get along, but he definitely full-on despises Liam. I've always assumed that something happened between them that Hunter hasn't seen fit to share.

"I don't hate him. We're just not friends."

I don't ask anything else about it, because it feels like I'm putting him on the spot in a way I don't mean to. I watch water striders skim across the surface of the river's edge. The water is calm here, below the reservoir. I've always loved the hot summer days I've spent at the river with my friends and family. I hate that it's making me so stressed to be near it now. This river valley feels like a trap. Like a tomb. When am I going to get over this? What will it take?

"Hey, are you okay?" Grace asks, gripping my wrist loosely.

"Yeah, I'm fine. I'm just a little weird around rivers and reservoirs right now, that's all."

"Understandable," says Tera. "You should have told us!"

"No, I need to get over it."

"You don't need to get over anything until you're ready to get over it," says Liam.

Surprised, I meet his gaze. He strikes me more as a "walk it off" kind of guy. Mainly because that's how he is on the soccer field.

"I feel fine with all of you here," I tell them. "But I had a hard time crossing the bridge on the way over."

"Oh, I'll drive you home when you're ready," says Roman. "Or we can all walk with you across the bridge. Whatever you want to do."

I fight against the feeling that I don't want them to be extra nice to me. The way Roman looks at me right now, it's almost desperate. Like he's begging me to let him do this. It hits me how maybe it isn't that they suddenly think I'm weak or delicate but that my accident scared them and they need to channel that helpless feeling into something productive.

"That would be great," I say. "Thank you."

We keep walking along the river, and the farther I go, the calmer I feel. The embankment is steep enough that it feels like a whole separate world down here. Sounds of traffic are muted, homes barely visible behind tree-lined banks. I find myself falling back a little from my friends again, alone with Liam.

I suspect from Tera's frequent casual glances that it's intentional this time. Grace doesn't look back once.

"How's your investigation?" Liam asks.

"Oh, I planned to use today to try to rule out a person from my list, but . . . I'm here instead."

"You're still working on it, though? Or planning to?"

"Yeah." I stop walking. Look up at him. He hasn't asked me who's on the list, but he *has* to be curious. "Why? You think I shouldn't?"

"No, I think you should." He shoves his hands in his pockets. "If it were me, I wouldn't be able to stop digging till I found something. And I . . . like that you're that way, too."

I don't know how to react to that. Is it flirting? It feels like flirting.

"I think you should go to that Halloween party," I tell him.

And with a smile, I turn away from him and start walking again.

Hunter's back when I get home. When I ask him how his soccer workout went, he says it was fine. I don't mention Liam. I'll keep that little tidbit and pull it out if and when I decide I need to know exactly what he was up to today. I do, however, make a mental note to add him to my Suspicious People list. If they lie to me, they're on there. I can't afford to be sentimental about this. Even if Hunter's never given me a real reason not to trust him.

"Mom and Dad went to do game night at Aunt Jenna's," Hunter tells me. "You wanna get pizza? I can go pick it up."

"I don't know. There's not any leftovers?" One of the downsides of where we live is that literally no one delivers here. And other than a brick oven pizza food truck sometimes during the summer, our closest pizza option is in St. Elm. It's kind of annoying.

"There's the salmon from last night."

I make a disgusted face. "Pizza it is. I'll order it; you throw out the salmon and make it look like we ate it."

When I pull out my phone, I notice I've got an unread text. I figure it's from Sky since I haven't heard from her all day, but it isn't. It's a number I don't recognize—one that my phone flags as *suspected spam*.

The message chills my blood: Just let it go, Amelia.

"What's up?" Hunter asks, seeing my puzzled expression.

I show him the text. "I think it's not meant for me. I mean, it's not even an 802 or a 603 number. What state does 583 belong to?"

"I don't know. But the message is clearly meant for you. It has your *name*."

My heart beats faster. "Maybe it's, like, a prank or something?"

Hunter's lips thin. "We should just have cereal for dinner. And maybe we should call Mom and Dad, have them come home."

"I don't want to call Mom and Dad. Please don't call them. You know they'll get all worked up, and I don't want that."

"Then what *do* you want? Amelia, this text message is not a joke; it's a threat."

"Or it's advice." I feel backed into a corner. It's one thing to believe someone hurt me and another thing to have proof of it. I don't want this to be proof. "I mean, Sky's always telling me I should let my life get back to normal, and she doesn't even know I'm thinking any of this. Maybe someone else feels that way, too."

"So one of your friends got a burner phone and sent you this threatening text instead of just saying that to your face?" Hunter folds his arms and gazes levelly at me. "In that case, get new friends. And I'm asking again: If you don't want to tell Mom and Dad about this, what do you want to do?"

"I want . . . I want to forget about all of it. I want to be a normal person again."

"So you're going to . . . *let it go*, as the message advises? Like that girl in *Frozen*?"

I nod, even though I'm pretty sure I'm lying. I don't think I *can* let it go. "I'm not sure the girl in *Frozen* and I are quite the same. But as long as you promise not to sing the song, then . . . yeah. That's what I'm going to do."

"Okay. Then I won't say anything to Mom and Dad. But keep me in the loop if you get more weird messages, all right? And I don't want— Please let's just have cereal for dinner."

"Cereal sounds great. I'm starving, anyway."

Hunter visibly relaxes when I don't fight him on this, and I *know* he's not the one who tried to kill me, not the one who sent the threatening text, but even still . . . where was he today? And why did he lie? What if my brother is involved somehow and I can't trust him after all? I don't know what I'd do. Some days I hate my brother more than I love him. Some days I'm so annoyed that I can't stand for him to even breathe in my direction. He's my worst enemy as often as he's my closest friend. But no matter what, I've always trusted him, and I hate that he's lying to me about something. Even if what he's lying about is probably nothing of consequence. I don't want any doubts. Not about Hunter, of all people.

I eat my cereal so fast I barely taste it, then excuse myself to my room so I can be alone with my thoughts. I *do* want to forget about it, and I *should* forget about it, but I can't. I need to figure out who sent me this text message. I try calling the phone number. No one answers, of course. The voicemail's generic. It just tells me to leave a message for the number in a digitized voice. I type the number into a search engine, and it spits out the name of some random town in Nebraska. I don't know anyone from Nebraska, and the town's got a couple thousand residents. Not much bigger than here. I even pay a semi-sketchy website for more details, but it's a waste of money. The only added detail it provides is that it's a cell phone number—which seems obvious—and that it's associated with some pay-by-the-month service I've never heard of. When I look that up, I discover that it's one where you can basically pick your entire phone number. Which means this call could have come from *anyone*. Even if they've never visited Nebraska in their life.

So I've learned something, but I've also learned nothing. I add the phone number to the evidence page Liam started in my notebook and then reluctantly add Hunter's name to my

Suspicious People list. It's discouraging to add a name without removing any. I move to cross off Clarissa but realize that maybe I *shouldn't*. She's always hated me, and she sure didn't have much good to say about Maria.

Feeling a little melancholy now, I fold myself into the chair next to my bedroom window and peer out. My room faces the road. It doesn't really matter because we only get traffic from people who live on our road or who have been led astray by their GPS systems or who are taking ATVs up onto the mountain. My brother's room has a more serene view, though, facing the field behind our house, with the trees off to one side and the back of the development visible from afar. That's where Sky lives, and even though we're on completely separate roads, I still think of her as my neighbor. She can be at my house in about two minutes when she crosses that field.

But I can see woods, too, if I look past Mr. Omerton's house. And the mountain. I lean my head against the window frame and try to focus on that, on the peacefulness of the outdoors and the trees and our quiet little world. But all I can think about is the strange number and Hunter's lie and why Sky hasn't texted me all day, and now there's a curtain moving in one of the upstairs rooms of Mr. Omerton's house, and his face appears. He's watching me. Again.

I haven't told my parents how creepy he's been lately. I've started keeping my blinds closed more often than not so I don't have to deal with it. The feel of his eyes on me makes my skin crawl, but now I'm paranoid about everything, so I don't move away from the window immediately. I try to look natural by first holding up my phone like I've just received a message, and then I get up and move to the corner, where he can't see me.

Maybe I should have let Hunter say something to Mom and Dad about the weird text message. It was true, what I said: I *do* want to forget about all this and be a normal person again. But it's never not on my mind, and I'm starting to feel completely paranoid.

What are u up to? Come hang out. I text Sky, even though it's the fourth message I've sent her today and she has yet to reply to any of them.

OMG so sorry I ignored u all day!! Her reply is surprisingly immediate, followed by: I can't come over rn but we need to do something soon.

Yeah ok just tell me when you're free?? You've been so busy lately.

I feel like my text sounds needy and whiny, but honestly, what is up with her?

I know, I'm sorry. I'll try to do better.

I don't know what response I was looking for, but I do know this wasn't it.

8

Pyrrharctia isabella. That's the Latin name for the woolly bear caterpillar, which becomes an isabella tiger moth. It's one of my favorite insects, in both moth and caterpillar form, and right now I'm watching one such fuzzy caterpillar trek across my driveway. The orange band that circles the middle of its body is wide, which supposedly means we'll have a mild winter, but the other day I saw one with an extremely narrow orange band, so I'm not sure how reliable these things are as weather predictors.

They are, however, extremely resilient. During the winter, woolly bear caterpillars freeze solid, and when the weather warms up, they thaw out and go about their business. This is an insect fact people seem to find interesting rather than repulsive. Most of the insect facts I share have the opposite effect, which is by choice—I have a tiny bit of a mean streak and enjoy grossing people out sometimes. It's funny, anyway, which insects people find disgusting and which ones they don't. Caterpillars are larvae just like maggots, but maggots have associations with rotting things, and sometimes caterpillars are fuzzy and colorful. There's a metaphor in that, probably.

The front door bursts open, and Mom emerges from the house. She looks totally frazzled. "Amelia, thank God. Come help me."

I don't move. "With what?"

"I'm making decorations for the party next week, and I'm in way over my head. *Help*."

"This does not sound like what I want to do with my Sunday afternoon." As I'm saying it, though, I'm already getting up. My knee crackles like an elderly person's. "Why can't Dad help you?"

"Dad's pricing winter tires so he and all his drivers won't die this winter."

I follow her indoors. Spending thousands of dollars on winter tires for all his trucks is *probably* less fun than helping Mom with whatever insane ideas she found on Pinterest for their annual adults-only Halloween party. Though at least Dad's *invited* to the party.

Our living room and kitchen are both impressive disasters considering that I've been outside for only a couple of hours. Half-filled fake blood bags and half-empty bottles of juice sit on the counter. There are balloons encased in thick string all over the barstools (and floor). Empty toilet paper rolls on the table, inexplicably. Pallets on the living room floor. Fake spiders spilling all over the couch. Bottles of paint. Bins of Halloween decorations. Fake spiderwebs. Newspaper. Unused balloons. Candy.

"Did a Halloween store throw up in here?" I ask.

"Don't start. I need you to *very carefully* pop all those balloons and then hot glue some of these spiders onto the outside. Like this." She shows me a picture of a pretty string lantern on her phone. "They're going on the porch, and I'm going to put glow lights in them."

"Okay . . ." I pick up one of the balloons and just . . . stare at it for a long moment. "Mom, how, exactly, are you expecting me to do this with one functional hand?"

"Oh. Right." She frowns thoughtfully. "Well, instead, maybe you could start emptying out the Halloween bins? And help me pin up some of the decorations."

This feels much more doable, so I start in. We work quietly, me emptying the bins and Mom piping juice and alcohol into the rest of the fake blood bags. I've been waiting to be alone with her, and since Hunter's off who knows where again today, now's my chance. But the problem is, I don't exactly know what to say.

"Hey, Mom?" I start, then hesitate. "Can I ask you something?"

"Anything." She peels a blood-type sticker off a sheet and presses it onto one of the blood bags.

"Well, I just . . . The other day at school, I heard someone in the bathroom speculating that Maria Lugen might have . . . that she died on purpose. Like, you know . . . jumped."

Mom frowns. The next sticker goes on much less gently. "I guess I'm not surprised. People always do that, don't they? Form reckless conclusions and then start rumors without thinking about the impact of what they're saying."

"Yeah, it's not great. But it made me wonder . . . I hadn't really thought . . ." I pull a glow-in-the-dark cat out of the bin and hold it to my chest. "When I had my accident, did you think that I . . . ?"

I don't know why I can't say it. Why the word *suicide* snags in my throat.

Mom puts down the page of stickers and comes closer. "It crossed my mind, because how could it not? But I didn't really ever think that, no."

"It was Clarissa," I say, blinking back tears. "She's the one who was talking about Maria in the bathroom at school. And before I came out of the stall, she said the same thing about me."

Mom takes the glow-in-the-dark cat from my arms, and then she hugs me tight. "That must have been really hard to hear."

I nod into her shoulder, still trying to hold back tears because I don't even know what I'm so emotional about. "I hated the way they were talking about it, like it was so *interesting*. Like Maria wasn't even a real person, and just like . . . fascinated at the idea of someone committing suicide without thinking about what that really means."

Mom hugs me tighter, and she doesn't say anything else.

None of us noticed it really, when Hunter first started showing signs of depression. It was small stuff like moodiness and lethargy, and my parents chalked it up to puberty, while I was too young to understand the intricacies of mental health. But one day shortly after my twelfth birthday, Hunter asked me if I ever felt like being alive was just too much work, and although I didn't know exactly *what*, I knew at once that something was wrong. I told Mom, who called Dad, who came home immediately, and Hunter went to therapy for the first time the very next day.

He was furious with me for two weeks, but after that, he told me I'd saved him. It's probably part of why we continue to be not just siblings but also friends. We trust each other, rely on each other. My stomach twists as I think of Hunter's name on my Suspicious People list.

For the first time in our entire lives, I cannot trust my brother.

"If I could shield you from all the crappy things people will say about you in your life, I would," Mom tells me. "But unfortunately there will always be Clarissas in this world, and you're still going to be navigating stuff like that even when you're my age. But what she thinks isn't what matters. Your dad and I know this was just a terrible accident, and if we thought anything else, we would already have taken steps to protect you. I hope you know that."

"I do." I smile at her. "I really do, Mom."

"Good." She ruffles my hair. "I'm glad we had this talk. You've been a little closed off, you know."

"I know. I'm sorry. It's all been a lot."

"I'm sure it has. And you've been handling it admirably."

She goes back to her work with the fake blood bags, and I return to emptying the Halloween bins.

It's nice that she thinks I'm handling things admirably, but I'm not sure that's true. In fact, I know it isn't. Here I am, fixating on finding out the truth about what happened to me at the expense of my relationships and my trust and everything good about my life.

Guilt needles me. Whether it was clumsiness or something more sinister, I almost died. And as awful as that feels on my end, I was unconscious when I was found. My death, had it happened, would have been so easy and peaceful. I would have floated off to whatever comes next without any pain or suffering to speak of. But the suffering I would have left in my wake is immeasurable. I've been pretty wrapped up in my own thoughts about all this, and I haven't stopped to think—*really* think—how my parents must feel. It's one of those universal truths that parents are supposed to die before their children, and when the opposite happens, it's devastating. They shouldn't have been forced to face my mortality yet, and they were. They still are; my cast and my dizzy spells and all the rest of it are constant reminders of what happened.

I should make things easier on them, and on Hunter and on myself. I should stop trying to solve an unsolvable mystery and I should move forward with my life. I should *just let it go*, as the mystery text instructed.

Unfortunately, all that's much easier said than done.

9

I know the Liam crush situation is getting more serious because when I head to my free period on Tuesday, nerves and excitement spark in my stomach. There's an interesting-looking moth on the door of the library when I arrive, and usually I'd stop here and take pictures of it and try to figure out what kind it is. But today all I can think about is seeing Liam and telling him about the text message from Saturday.

He's not here.

My heart sinks, and I feel dumb. He never promised we would spend every free period together, and he doesn't owe me anything. It's my own fault I feel let down.

I slump into one of the faux leather chairs near the front of the library and pout. Honestly can I not have *one* thing go my way?

The universe rewards pouting, apparently, because about thirty seconds later, Liam shows up. He spots me immediately, and a smile lights his face. There's something truly exhilarating about knowing someone's excited to see you when you're also excited to see them.

He beelines straight for me, sits in the chair next to mine, and sets his backpack on the floor at his feet.

"You look like you have something to tell me," he says. He's leaned into the corner of the chair, body angled toward mine, arm resting on the back of the seat.

"I might." I clutch my notebook tight for a second, but then I spill the whole story about the text message and the burner phone with a Nebraska area code. "So I didn't learn anything. But I did get to at least, like, *do* something."

"Finding your calling?" He grins at me, and I don't like that I can't tell if he's being real or teasing.

"Yeah, no. I'll stick to studying bugs. Their actions always make sense, you know? People are totally unpredictable and illogical, and I don't think I'd want a career where you have to delve deep into the ones that are even more unpredictable than average."

He chuckles at that. "I'm with you there. People are a disaster."

His weight shifts and his knee touches mine. I hold very still, like a spooked deer.

"I guess I did learn one thing, though," I say. "I learned that someone definitely did try to hurt me. No one would have sent me that text if not."

Such a simple statement, but I hope he can't tell how

terrified it makes me to admit it. Part of me still thinks this is all in my head, an elaborate scam my concussed brain has schemed up. But the evidence that I should trust my instincts sure is piling up.

Liam frowns. "Are you afraid?"

Such a simple question, and the obvious answer—*yes*—slips to the edge of my tongue, but it stops there. "Sometimes." That's the honest answer. "I think— It's really hard to be scared all the time. Holding on to fear is just . . . it's exhausting, and it's hard to do when there's not an active threat. What I feel is more just this constant awareness of my own mortality, and a paranoia about every single person around me. That probably doesn't make any sense."

"No, it does." He adjusts the angle of the backpack at his feet. "Have you ruled anyone out yet?"

I shake my head. "Only the people who weren't on there to begin with. And, I mean, they're only ruled out until they make me change my mind."

"Ruthless."

"I can be." I grin at him. "You've been warned."

"I will beware of getting on your bad side." He pauses. "*Or* your suspicious list."

I curl my fingers tighter around the notebook, instinctively. I'm sure he's dying of curiosity as I would be, but I cannot show him this list. I don't want him to see the names of my brother and best friend and wonder how truly untrusting I am.

"Don't you worry about my list," I say lightly. "It takes some work to get on there. You have to give me a good reason to mistrust you."

"That's pretty much the opposite of everything in my plans," he says, and my fingertips tingle with nerves.

After that, the conversation moves away from my notebook and my suspicious people, and it's just kind of flirty. I've never had a free period go by so fast, and when he leaves for his Spanish class, I wish I could go with him.

I start to pack up my notebook, and I think about the list of names on its first page. Determination pits in my chest. I shove it into my bag and pull out my phone.

I need to see u, I text Sky. Then, I have to know what's up. If somethings changed in our friendship then ok but you've gotta let me in on it. I need it all out in the open. Tell me whatever it is. I don't even care, I just want to know. Please.

It is the most desperate and pathetic text I've ever sent, but it's honest. She doesn't reply right away, and it stresses me out even though I know she's in class. I stay in the library an extra five minutes after I should have left for my next class, and still nothing. Will I have to have a confrontation with her in the car on the way home? I extremely hope not.

Finally, just as I slip into my desk—the last person to enter the classroom—my screen lights up. Class is starting, but I risk a glance anyway.

Ur right we should talk. Take ur atv up to the screen tonight??

I text back a simple ok, but my heart is in my throat. So

there *is* something. The thought of going to the screen alone with her actually terrifies me. Not knowing what she's going to say, and this nagging worry that's been plaguing me with her for months, going alone to the screen—on top of the mountain, poised nicely on a ledge—seems like a bad, bad idea.

But I'm going to do it anyway, because I'm desperate and I need to know where I stand with my best friend.

I want Sky off my list, and it'll happen tonight.

One way or another.

10

"I don't know how I feel about this," Mom says, holding the key to our RZR tight in her fist.

Dad's sitting on the couch pretending to have no interest, because I asked him first, hoping for an easier yes, and he said, "Ask your mother."

He's not usually home midweek, but one of his drivers had faulty actuator wiring, so he swapped trucks, and he's stubbornly fixing the broken one himself in his shop. He was out there when I got home, swearing quite creatively at the vehicle, but he followed me in after I asked about the ATV. He's curious what Mom will say, I think.

"You know I'll be careful," I plead. "I'm always careful."

Mom's lips purse, and I know she's thinking, *Well, except that one time.*

"Fine," she says. "I can tell by your father's complete silence that he thinks I should let you go, so . . ."

"I would have said yes to it," says Dad, finally glancing over the back of the couch at Mom. "But to be fair, I say yes to everything."

I can tell Mom wants to make a gross joke in response to that, and I'm so glad she restrains herself.

"Skylar has to drive. You're still not cleared. And tell her to be *very careful*," she says, pressing the key into my palm but not letting it go yet. "And don't go on any of the steep paths; stick to the gentler ones. *Do not* go to the screen, it's too— I don't need you near any ledges. It's starting to get dark earlier now, remember."

"I remember." I close my fist around the key. "And I will let Sky drive."

We go to the screen.

Technically, I never promised not to, and Mom should be glad this is as rebellious as it gets for me.

The screen is exactly what it sounds like: a huge white screen. It's not that different from the ones you see at a drive-in. It's all metal, and to be honest, I have no clue what it's for because I've never asked. It just sits here on top of the mountain, covered in graffiti that you can't see looking at the mountain from afar but can see all too well up close. It's reachable via a rocky trail you can traverse with an ATV—or by hiking, if you're feeling ambitious.

People have been coming up here for a long, long time, for all sorts of reasons. I like it here for the same reason I like— liked—walking out behind the dam: the view. My house, my road, the Connecticut River, and Vermont's mountains all sprawl before me in full autumn splendor. It's almost more beautiful in the fading golden light of dusk than during the day. Looking down at the world below makes me feel so peaceful. My hometown has always felt like a haven to me. It isn't perfect, of course. Some of us could stand to get out of here once in a while and meet other people who aren't exactly like us, and small-town gossip can get pretty brutal. But it has always felt so safe. A lot of people don't even lock their doors still, or don't even *have* locks.

I don't feel safe anymore, and I hate that that feeling was taken from me. I still don't trust my instincts, but even if I'm wrong about what happened to me, I still lost that sense of security. Maybe it was naive to hang on to that feeling for so long, to think I was untouchable by anything bad in this world because I live in a small town, because I know full well that's not true. And maybe it's good for me to let go of that innocence, to peel back the glamour from my world and see it for what it truly is, both the good and the ugly.

Sky doesn't like sitting on the ground because ants creep her out, so while I sit on a rock with my knees pulled to my chest, she leans against one leg of the screen. I let an ant roam onto my finger and watch it scurry over my skin with its quick legs and its constantly roving antennae.

"What if it bites you?" Sky says.

"It won't."

"You are such a weird, brave person." She sighs.

"Am I?" I lower my arm back to the rock and watch the confused ant scurry gratefully back to more familiar terrain. "Brave, I mean?"

"I wouldn't hold an ant, or a spider, or any bug at all for that matter."

"I've just never really thought about it, you know? Whether I'm brave or I'm not or whether it even matters."

"I guess bravery is in the eye of the beholder, isn't it?" Sky comes and sits tentatively beside me on the rock, like she's proving herself brave. "Like, I'm afraid of bugs, so I think it's really brave that they don't even bother you. But I'm not afraid of snakes, so when someone picks one up, I'm like, who even cares?"

"I think it's probably just about doing things that scare you, no matter what those things are. And I don't know. I just don't know if I'm brave or not. Sometimes I am, I guess."

"Same." Sky inhales deeply, shakily. I can practically feel her vibrating with nerves. "And on that note . . . it's time for me to tell you . . . the thing I have to tell you."

"Yeah?" I don't look at her, like she's a skittish animal I'm trying not to spook. "What's that?"

"I don't think you'll be mad about it. But if you are, I think . . . maybe only because how long I—we—I waited to tell you."

I do look at her then, pushing my glasses higher on my nose while she chews aggressively on a thumbnail.

"Hunter and I are dating."

"You . . . and Hunter. My brother?"

She nods.

"For how long?"

"Since the Fourth of July."

"That's almost four months, Sky! Why didn't you say anything?"

"Because it's weird!" She pulls the sleeves of her shirt over her hands and holds them there in fists, one of her stress habits. "I'm at your house all the time, I felt like I should see him as just, like, a brother or something. And for a long time, I did, I guess. He was just sort of there, like a friendly piece of furniture. But then somewhere along the way I started noticing that he was cute, and I guess he felt the same. But until we knew if it was going to stick, at least for a little while, we didn't want to say anything. I didn't want it to have a negative effect on our friendship, and . . . Anyway, that's what I was going to tell you that day, at the dam. And then after . . . it was really hard. I can't tell how you're taking all this, Amelia, and I just . . . Neither Hunter nor I wanted to pile on any more crap than you've already got happening."

"I kind of . . . wish you had." I don't know how I feel about this. It is completely unexpected, and I'm upset she didn't feel like she could tell me, but I'm also relieved. I've been worried about her secret since before my accident, and this explains everything. "Is that why you've been so distant? And why both of you were MIA last weekend? You were hanging out?"

She nods. "And I shouldn't have ignored your texts all day. But I didn't want to come up with some lie, either, like I know Hunter did."

"A really bad lie. I knew he was hiding something from me when Liam showed up at Roman's."

Sky rolls her eyes. "He is the worst liar, and I told him he shouldn't try it."

"Does anyone else know about you?"

"Not unless they guessed it, which I doubt. We've been pretty good, haven't we?"

"Depends how you define *good*."

Sky hooks her arm around mine and looks up at me anxiously. "Are you mad?"

"No. I'm not mad. I wish you'd told me. I *really* wish you had. But if you want to date my brother . . . well, he couldn't do better."

She laughs. "What about me?"

"*You* could do better, of course." I lean my head against hers. "Just keep the PDA to a minimum in my presence, okay?"

She laughs again. A relieved, cheerful sound. "I think that's fair."

We sit in silence for a long moment after that, and then she asks me, "How are you doing?"

"Fine. I mean, it's slightly disturbing that my best friend finds my gross brother attractive enough to date, but—"

"No, not about that. About, you know, everything. Life postaccident."

"Oh, that." I look at the view before us, the leaves at peak color. It's beautiful, but it's death. It's trees shedding down to the bare minimum to survive winter. Making themselves smaller, emptier, so they can cling on through the tough times ahead. "I feel . . . shaken. My world is different now, and I don't want it to be."

"I know what you mean. You almost died, and I almost lost my best friend. It's not something I ever imagined in my wildest nightmares." She hugs me tight, and my eyes sting with tears. "It was awful when I found you, you know."

"I'm sure it was."

Sky hasn't talked about this with me—at all. She hasn't been talking to me about anything. Maybe she has Hunter for that now, I realize, with a pinch in my gut. She's known him so long, it was probably easy to slip into a relationship when he was someone she could confide in right away. I'm glad she had that, while I was recovering, but I don't like the thought that she needs me less because of it.

She leaves an arm around me and gazes out at the rapidly darkening sky. It's so quiet up here, there's no people noise, only the rattle of a gentle breeze through crisp leaves and the rustle of squirrels and mice and whatever else scurrying about. It's almost funny how I'm sitting here on a ledge in the near dark surrounded by forest and I feel completely unafraid. Wildlife could hurt me, but it doesn't *want* to hurt me. A black bear would rather destroy a nice full bird feeder than my skinny body. Animals are just trying to survive. People are the ones who disturb me.

"Tell me about it," I request. "Tell me about that day. Like, all of it. I mean, I don't even know what made you decide to tell me then, finally."

"Well, I . . ." She bites her lip. This must be difficult for her, but I need to hear it. "It was *hard*, keeping it from you. I hated it. It made sense at first, but then it started to feel weird and wrong, and Hunter was being such a ball of panic about it. The longer it went, the more worried he was that you were going to be mad. I think he figured I would break up with him if you didn't like the idea, or if you were hurt that we didn't tell you or whatever. Finally, I just decided screw it, and I texted you that Friday and asked if we could meet at our spot the next afternoon. You were working on that group chemistry project after school, so I caught Hunter before practice and told him what I'd decided. We had a big fight. Well, a *quiet* fight because we didn't want anyone to hear us, but, like, furious whispering at the top of the swimming pool stairwell. He was mad that I'd decided without him, and he wanted to participate. I told him this was a conversation for you and me, and that if he didn't respect that, there would be nothing to tell you at all because we wouldn't be together anymore. He accepted it, but we, like, weren't speaking that night, and I'm not sure how long our silent treatment would have lasted if you hadn't, well, you know."

"You're welcome," I say, in a terrible attempt to lighten the mood.

"I almost chickened out. I didn't really want to tell you about it while I was so mad at him, you know, like, 'Hey, I'm dating your brother but at the moment I kind of hate him so what do you think about that?'" She laughs a little, and so do I. "But I went, and I saw that your car was parked at the beach, so I parked next to you and walked back behind the dam, and you . . . weren't there. I went farther along the road to see if maybe you were, like, walking around while you waited for me, but you weren't around the bend anywhere either, so I went back to our usual spot. And that's when . . ."

She swallows hard, and her voice is softer when she continues. "I saw some broken branches and then I saw . . . I saw *you*, crumpled, partway down the bank. All I could really see was your sweater, but I've seen you wear that purple sweater so many times. I called to you, and you didn't say anything. I screamed, and still nothing. I stood there for probably like a full entire minute just . . . totally panicking before I took off, ran back to my car, and drove partway up the hill to that spot where there's service. I called 911, and once I knew they were on their way, I went back. I paced in front of that guardrail, looking at the broken branches and your purple sweater and—" Her voice breaks. "See, this is why I haven't talked about this. I'm getting upset, and I shouldn't *be* upset. I'm not the one who got hurt."

I lean my head on her shoulder. "You didn't get hurt the same way I did, but you *did* get hurt. I'm so sorry you had to see that. It must have been so— I can't imagine if our roles had been reversed, how I would have felt. What I would have done."

"The worst part was that I couldn't go down there. I knew if I tried to get to you, I'd end up falling. And then watching the paramedics . . . I was so scared they would drop you, and I had no idea if you were dead or alive. None of us did, until they got you back up the hill. But at the same time they were talking about how quick they had to be because if you woke up, you could have startled yourself and fallen the rest of the way. It was so . . . I hate it. I hate that this happened to you."

I feel numb inside. Not an empty numbness but the kind where whatever emotion I'm feeling is too much for me so instead I feel nothing.

"Let's not dwell on this," I tell her, and I jump to my feet. My brain and my still-sore ribs protest the sudden movement. "Let's take the RZR and drive around the mountain for a while and just, like, feel alive."

I reach out my hand and pull Sky up. Her eyes shine with unshed tears, but I can tell she wants to stop thinking about this, too, and just feel alive for a little while.

So that's exactly what we do.

It's pitch-black when we get home, though it's only nine o'clock. Mom's unimpressed, but we're fine, so she doesn't say much. I eat the leftover steak and potatoes she offers me and then go up to my room and pull my notebook out of my backpack. My head throbs with a dull headache from bouncing around in the ATV, and the numbness from earlier lingers in my heart.

With a small, satisfied smile, I draw a heavy line through two names on my list: Skylar Stewart and Hunter Stern.

And then the dam breaks on my emotional numbness, and

a potent blend of sorrow and loss and joy and relief and pain and guilt and rage floods my veins. It burns in my heart, and I am overwhelmed. I let myself sit with the feeling, something I haven't done since I left the hospital. Even when I think about what happened, I haven't let myself truly *feel* what happened, and I need to. I need to let the pain cut me so I can get past this. I sit for a long, long while, just living in my emotion.

And, finally, I start to cry.

11

I am not really a costume person. I like the spirit of Halloween—ghosts and monsters and bugs and gore—but costumes I'm just not good at. I never won the costume contest at the town hall as a little kid, and, to be honest, I never tried. Sky, on the other hand, always came up with something creative and homemade, and she often won.

The party tonight will be the first time everyone sees Sky and Hunter together as a couple, so it's a big deal for her. And weird for me.

Sky insisted that I wear a costume that I can only describe as a sexy corpse witch, complete with pale foundation to make me look even whiter than normal (who knew that was possible!) and heavy black shadow around my eyes. She and my brother are both zombies, decorated in grotesque fake wounds and horrifying makeup.

I have to admit, I enjoyed watching my brother grumble and give in about the makeup and the wounds. He's about as ambitious as I am when it comes to costumes, usually.

"I don't think it's fair that you get to wear shapeless rags and I have to wear a dress," I complain when we approach Alec's driveway.

"You'll thank me later," she says deviously. "I think . . . certain people at the party will like it."

Hunter's eyes meet mine in the rearview mirror and narrow. "What people?"

"*You* don't need to worry about that, now do you?" Sky pats his arm.

"Yeah, I'll let you know when I need you to activate protective-big-brother mode. Till then, chill."

"We'll see," he says, but doesn't press.

"I'm just happy Sky convinced you to come as something other than a Fortnite character," I say, scrambling for a subject change.

Hunter laughs. "Next year."

Sky says something in response, but I don't hear it because I've been overcome with that weird feeling again like I had after Liam laughed in the library. The intense suspicion that while I was falling, someone was *laughing*. Hunter's unlikely to spend Halloween with us next year; he'll be away at college. Thinking about his impending departure always puts me in a bad place. It's yet another thing about my life that's changing, and I've had a harder time with it since my accident.

Knowing this makes me wonder if the memory of laughter is even real or if it's just something my brain's doing to compensate for all its confusion.

"Still with us back there?" Hunter asks.

"Oh, yeah, sorry." I smile weakly, but I'm glad when he pulls to a stop and we get out of the car.

We have to park at the bottom of the very long driveway because there are already so many people here. I'm glad my parents have their own Halloween party, because I think it would be weird to go to one together with them that was at someone else's house.

Tera, Roman, and Grace meet us partway up the driveway. Tera and Roman are dressed as scarecrows, and Grace is a skeleton. Full face paint and skintight skeleton suit and all. I can't even bring myself to look directly at her, which is all I need to say about how well she's pulling off such a daring outfit.

"Thank God," she says, looping her arm through mine. "Third wheels unite."

I laugh.

"Your costume looks great, by the way," she adds.

"So does yours. Did you do your own face paint? It's amazing."

She beams. "Listen, you don't get this good at Halloween overnight. I've been practicing for years."

"True, but you still have to have more artistic skill than I possess to get it right, I think."

"You did fine." She pauses, scrutinizing my face. "Liam will definitely be interested."

I swallow against a sensation of disappointment. I don't mind anyone else pushing me toward Liam, but I do seem to mind it with her. "Thanks," I say softly. "I hope so."

Alec's parents have gone all out on the decor. The lawn in front of their big log cabin is decorated with all manner of animatronics—corpses rising from coffins, ghosts hovering, cackling witches, even a cocooned corpse. Their wraparound porch features flashing orange and black lights woven between rails and bats and spiders hanging from the eaves. Their windows are all coated with spooky window hangings, and the word *beware* drips across the front door in fake blood.

"This. Is. Amazing." Grace pulls out her phone to photograph the scene. "Even my mom will be impressed."

She starts typing, I assume sending the pictures in a text to her mom.

"Is your whole family into Halloween?"

"My dad could take it or leave it, but my mom is worse than me." She holds out her phone to show me a picture of a beautiful adult version of herself wearing a very elaborate spider costume. "This is her costume tonight."

"No offense, but this is my new favorite costume."

"I thought you might feel that way. She actually loves bugs, just like you."

"Really?" There are so many things I don't know about Grace's family and her life. Because I've only ever known her here and it's so easy to forget that she has this whole other world she's part of. "Do you miss them when you're at school?"

"Yeah. But I'm glad I'm here. I'm *definitely* a city girl, don't get me wrong, but it's nice to be in the country, too. It's good to remember that not everyone has everything they want right at their fingertips all the time, and that there's nothing wrong with that. Plus it's so pretty here, of course." She smiles wryly. "They were very smug when I told them they were right to send me to the academy, though. I fought it pretty hard at first."

"I can imagine." I push open the door to the house, and we are met with a burst of music and laughter and voices. "You went from New York City to the complete middle of nowhere, and it's full of the very whitest people."

She throws back her head and laughs. I admire the skeleton makeup that continues down her throat and lines up perfectly with her costume, stark white against her dark skin.

She catches me staring, and for a moment we're awkward again.

But then Liam appears.

"Hey," he says, smiling. "I was wondering if you were actually going to show up or not."

"Oh, yeah, we're a little late. Sky insisted on doing my makeup."

"It looks good."

I blush, but luckily the lighting is dim for ambience.

"Hey, I'm going to go mingle, okay?" Grace winds an arm briefly around my waist. "There are more girls here than I expected, so I'm gonna go try my luck."

"I would wish you good luck, but you won't need it."

I watch her walk away, and then realize I'm doing it and pull my attention back to Liam. He's wearing a Jedi costume, which isn't the most creative, but it works. It makes me feel better about my costume, which looks great and all but isn't on par with the things my friends wore.

"So how long have you been here?" I ask.

"Half hour, maybe? Long enough to eat some crackers and cheese, and that's about it."

I look around, overwhelmed by how much there is to see. There's so many people wearing masks, I can't even tell who's my age and who's an adult.

"Are you hungry or anything?" he asks.

I shake my head. "I ate before I came. Something about everyone else digging around in buffet-style food just doesn't appeal to me."

"That surprises me, coming from you. Spiders, yes, but buffet, no?"

A smile curves my lips. "I am a mystery."

"Yeah." He takes a sip from the soda he's holding. "You are."

Alec approaches us. He's a senior, and he's friends with my brother, but, honestly, he's not one of my favorites. It's not that there's anything wrong with him; he's just one of those overly extroverted people who think all conversations live and die with them.

"Hi, Amelia," he says. "How's the cast?"

"Oh, it's great. I wish I could keep it forever," I say dryly.

"Liam, wouldn't have expected to see you here," Alec says, his tone distinctly less light.

"You did invite me, didn't you?" Liam's tone is just as unfriendly.

"I did invite the whole team, yeah."

I narrow my eyes. The implication that Liam isn't welcome despite being invited is pretty rude. Neither of them notices me, though. They're too busy glaring at each other.

Alec breaks the eye contact first, turning his attention back to me. "Hunter must be here somewhere, too, I'm guessing?"

I nod.

"Cool. I should find him and say hi. Want to help me?"

He asks the question casually, like he couldn't care less if I said no, but then he slings an arm around my shoulder as if that's something I remotely indicated I wanted. Beside me, Liam tenses, his hands balling into fists.

"No thanks," I say, and edge a step away from Alec so he's forced to remove the arm.

"You want to stay here with Liam?" His tone is skeptical.

"Yes." I fold my arms. "I do."

He stares at me for a long moment, then says, "Whatever. I'll go find Hunter. I'm sure he'll love hearing who you're hanging out with."

"I'm sure he will."

With no remaining options, Alec turns away and stalks off, presumably to find my brother. I sigh and turn back to Liam.

"I'm sorry about that," I tell him. "He's not actually interested in me. He just likes to win things."

"I know," says Liam. "Well, I guess I don't *know* because he could very well be interested in you, Amelia. But I mean, I know he likes to win things, and I know he didn't like that you're standing here with me."

"He was being very rude."

Liam shrugs. "I did tell you we're not friends."

There's a tension in the air between us now, and I'm starting to feel sweaty from all the bodies crammed into this house and from the discomfort of conflict.

"Are you hot?" I ask, which is a totally embarrassing thing to have said aloud, no matter how I meant it.

"Actually, yeah. They've got a gazebo thing out back, want to go there?"

"Absolutely."

He takes my hand as we weave through the crowd, and it makes me feel a different sort of heat. I spot a few people I know, including Alec's sister, Lydia, who waves and raises her eyebrows suggestively at me. I bite my lip to hide a smile. I don't know what's happening here, and I don't want to make it seem like something *is* if nothing comes of it.

A group of adults has already overtaken the gazebo, so we just start wandering. I stop near a shed on the outskirts of the property and nudge my toe against a soccer ball that sits there.

"I swear, every single one of you just lives and dies for soccer."

Liam shrugs. "I can't speak for everyone, but I feel like . . . I kind of have to, if I want a prayer at getting into a good college and not having to pay exorbitant student loans to go there."

"Please. You are athletic, smart, and well-spoken. Colleges will be fighting over you."

"You think?" He looks pleased.

"Yeah, I mean, you just used the word *exorbitant* casually in a sentence. I don't know what more evidence you need."

"Well, I like to be precise."

"Oh, I know." I look up at him, at his ocean-blue eyes and his chiseled face and his forever-tense shoulders, and suddenly I feel both bold and reckless. "I kind of . . . I want to know *precisely* what you think . . . about me."

"What I think about you." He repeats my words slowly, like he's digesting them, then smiles ever so slightly. "I think you're . . . sarcastic, and a little mean sometimes. But you're also not afraid to change your mind about things, even if it means disagreeing with people you care about. You're . . . Well, only someone who's a little bit odd would like insects as much as you do. You don't give up on things easily. You're very pretty. I . . . None of this is actually precise at all, because it's impossible to describe a person you're completely infatuated with, especially when you can't get a read on how they feel about you."

My stomach is filled with the wings of a thousand whirring dragonflies. "You're infatuated with me?"

He looks exasperated. "Have I really not made that clear?"

"I mean . . . I guess I didn't figure it was an accident I kept running into you," I say. "But I just— Why now? Why am I suddenly interesting?"

"You've always been interesting. But it hasn't always been my last year at this school, and you haven't always almost died."

He starts to look uncomfortable. He's telling me a whole lot about how he feels, and I've said absolutely nothing in return.

If our roles were reversed, I would be feeling painfully vulnerable right now. So I take a deep breath and a step closer. I rise to my toes, and without letting myself think about what I'm doing, I press my lips to his.

There's a brief moment when I think maybe this is a mistake, maybe he doesn't want me to kiss him at all, but then his arms are around me and he's kissing me back. I tangle my fingers in his hair, breathless and hungry and—for once—completely unconfused about what I want. He presses me back, gently, into the side of the shed and kisses me even harder, almost desperately. His hands are at my hips, holding me tight against him. It's a weird feeling to kiss this incredibly attractive person and know that, for whatever reason, he liked me first. He has liked me for a *while*. That thought burns hot inside of me.

I break the kiss when I start to get dizzy, but I press my face into the hollow of his throat, my good arm around his neck. We're quiet for a few moments, his hands trailing up and down my back. Then I say, hoarsely, "I, um, like you, too, if that was not made clear."

He laughs, and I feel the rumble of it against my cheek. I pull away from him, only a little, and ask, "So what happens now?"

"What *should* happen is that I ask you on a date. But that depends, I guess."

"On . . . ?"

He swallows hard. "If you're willing to tell . . . people."

"By 'people,' I assume you mean my brother." My stomach

flutters now with a different kind of nerves. I understand what he's asking. Am I willing to date him, publicly, even knowing that Hunter will be strongly opposed? I hesitate for a moment at the thought of it, but weirdly when I think about telling everyone, it's not my brother who makes me pause but Grace. Which is dumb. She doesn't like me the way Liam likes me, and she's my friend—she'll be happy for me. "I think— I don't think I care what he has to say about this."

Liam smiles and kisses me again, holding my face in both hands. "In that case, what are you doing Saturday night?"

12

Skylar insists that she help me prepare for my date on Saturday. I've been so excited about this since Halloween on Thursday, but I haven't wanted to admit it to anyone because it all seems . . . too easy. It isn't that I've never had a boyfriend before, or that no one's been interested, but Liam is so handsome, so put together, so quietly confident. He just seems very much out of my league.

As soon as Sky gets me into clothes she picked from her own closet—mine weren't good enough for such an important event, apparently—Hunter materializes, which complicates the getting-ready process.

"You can't wear that shirt," he says.

"That only makes me want to wear it more." I close my eyes so Sky can sweep something across the lids. "Subtle, remember," I tell her.

"I remember. Hold still. And Hunter, of course you hate her shirt. That's kind of your job."

He groans. "I can't believe you're doing this."

"Open your eyes now," Sky instructs me, and then turns to Hunter. "Quiet. Or you'll have to leave the room."

"I do like you when you're bossy." Hunter grins.

"Um, ew." I flinch when Sky starts tugging at my hair. "No flirting in my presence, thanks. Or I'll make you go back to pretending like you're not dating."

"Don't make her hair look too good, Sky," Hunter says, kicking at me. "We don't want him to know she put effort into this date."

"*We* don't?" I ask.

"Hunter, you really have to stop helping," says Sky. "Why don't you go downstairs and tell us when you see Liam pull in."

He wrinkles his nose but kisses her on the cheek and leaves.

"He doesn't want you to have a bad time," Sky says, inspecting me. "Maybe I'll even be able to convince him to like Liam more. He always listens to me when—"

"I do *not* want to hear the end of that sentence!"

"Sorry." She smiles. "Well, you look gorgeous. Promise you'll tell me *everything* when you get back?"

"I promise."

"He's here!" Hunter bellows up the stairs.

My stomach turns into a wasp's nest, and I bolt down the stairs. Mom and Hunter are both standing in the doorway; I can hear them talking to Liam, but I can't see him. Dad's gone since he was home most of the week, and it's too bad because he's so much less of a vulture than these two. I hop down the rest of the stairs and push through Mom and Hunter. Liam smiles at me, and I feel warm all over.

"I'll be home before eleven," I say when Mom opens her mouth.

"I was just going to say have fun," she tells me.

I smile at her. "Thanks. Bye."

I take Liam's hand and pull him away before they can talk to him more. I'm not worried about Mom, but Hunter is a different story.

"Where are you taking me?" I ask when we're in Liam's car.

"You'll see."

He keeps his secret the entire forty-five-minute car ride. When we finally stop, we're at the Insectarium they just built a few towns away from mine. Mom brought me when it first opened, but I haven't been since.

"How did you know I'd want to come here?" I ask, admiring the building. It's dusky out now, so it's not easy to see, but the exterior is painted in bright colors with butterflies and grasshoppers and dragonflies.

"Well, I had a suspicion. And Hunter might not like me, but he still told me you'd enjoy it, when I asked him."

Our first date has only just begun, and already it's the best one of my entire life.

The Insectarium's a big place, with two floors and several different rooms. We're practically alone; it's late enough that most people have already left. Liam seems wary of the insects, which is pretty adorable. He flat out refuses to go into the room with the spiders—he promises to wait outside the door while I look around.

I'd like to say that I exhibit totally normal, chill first-date behavior, but I do not. The fact that an Insectarium was built so close to where I live when nothing *ever* gets built near where I live is beyond my wildest hopes, and with this being only my second trip, the place still feels entirely magical.

After about an hour of telling Liam more than he probably ever wanted to know about bugs, I pause by a colorful mural.

"What do *you* like to do? I mean, besides soccer?"

"Well." He takes hold of my good hand. "Soccer is kind of my main thing, I guess. I like watching pro games and learning from what they do. I don't want to bank on soccer as a career, though. I'm not *that* good at it. I want to be an architect, I think. Because I like houses. I like looking at them, walking through them . . . I think I'd be good at designing them. I know that's weird."

"It's not weird. What colleges are you applying to?"

"A bunch of them, but if I get in, my first choice would be Dartmouth."

"Ambitious." My pulse races. "And not that far away."

"No." He brushes a stray bit of hair that's gotten caught in my glasses back from my face. "Not far away at all."

"I don't want to make you look at insects all night," I say, quelling the stupid happy feeling about him not wanting to go far away, "but I'm not ready to go home."

"What about ice cream?"

"Ice cream sounds awesome."

But he doesn't move. "Is it all right to kiss someone in an Insectarium?"

"I've never tried it." I pull him closer by a belt loop on his pants. "But what's the worst thing that could happen?"

"I guess we'll find out." He presses me gently against the mural and kisses me. He's *very* good at kissing. I wrap my good arm around his neck and completely lose myself in the sensation of the kiss.

A throat clears; an older man with a fuzzy beard glares at us from the doorway of the room. Liam steps away from me—very slowly. He takes my hand and leads me past the man, not even looking the slightest bit embarrassed. I, on the other hand, am mortified, although I'd do it again in an instant for another taste of that delicious shivery feeling I get from his touch.

We split a four-scoop brownie sundae from the Yummy Cow, a disturbingly named ice cream shop painted pumpkin orange with violet splotches that I think are meant to be cow spots. The sign out front glows neon green. It's supposed to be cow-shaped, but it actually looks like some sort of moose-alien hybrid.

They may be an epic failure in pretty much all areas of advertising, and their ice cream is only okay, but they're the only ones still open in November.

We eat in Liam's car at the park and ride just up the road. It's an unseasonably warm night, and way too many people were sitting at the tables outside the shop. Plus, as much as I like insects, I'm not a fan of them dive-bombing my face in the dark of night. Inside the car, I can appreciate the evening's beauty, the last smudges of purple fading to charcoal. Trees swaying like they're at a soft rock concert. Traffic whirring behind us, soothing white noise.

"So," I say, putting my feet up on the dashboard, "what is it that made you decide you wanted to date me?"

"Well, I kind of told you, didn't I? I've always noticed you. But you're also Hunter's sister, so I left it at noticing. Then I heard about you almost dying . . ." He twists his spoon hard in the ice cream, meeting my eyes. "You're lucky to be alive. You should have . . . well, you know. I wanted to talk to you when you came back to school, and when I finally ran into you twice in one day . . . it felt like fate. Or something."

"I've never completely understood what happened between you and Hunter. I know you have your middle school rivalry and whatever, but I feel like really you should be best friends."

"Soccer's the only thing your brother and I have in common."

He gets out of the car to dump the ice cream container in a trash can. I wonder if I've touched a nerve. It doesn't really seem like an explanation.

When he gets back in, he reaches across the space between our seats and takes my hand. "I don't completely know what happened, either. No offense, but he's always been kind of cocky."

"Be nice!" I interrupt. "Cocky, maybe, but he's a really good brother."

"I'm sorry. A little . . . overconfident."

I laugh. "Okay, just keep going."

"It got old when he kept pointing out how many goals he scored compared to how many I did when we were finally on the same team as freshmen. I'd been looking forward to it, honestly, seeing my biggest rival become my teammate, and I was disappointed when he didn't let the rivalry go. Anyway, I got sick of it, and one day during practice, I kicked a ball at his face. He wasn't even hurt, but he was pretty mad. And I think that was the end of any hope for us to become friends."

I imagine little ninth-grade Liam kicking a soccer ball at Hunter's face. I can't decide if I think it was a jerkish thing to do or not, but since it was three years ago, maybe I shouldn't mull it over too much.

"I know it's immature," he adds.

"You were young," I say, as though we aren't still both young. It doesn't seem like enough of an incident to have kept them enemies for so long. I know for a fact that Hunter has forgiven worse transgressions from other teammates. But there's always been something that kept Liam apart from the rest of his team, and sitting here looking at his handsome face, listening to him speak with measured grace, I have a hard time understanding it.

I stare at our intertwined fingers.

"What are you thinking about?" he asks.

I shrug. I don't want to say that I'm wondering why he doesn't get along with the rest of the team the way my brother does, but because I'm an idiot, I blurt out, "I don't know, just thinking about how apart you seem from the rest of your team, even when you're with them."

His eyes narrow and then smooth. "Is that a bad thing?"

"No," I say hurriedly. "I mean, I don't know. Depends how you feel about it, I guess."

"I'm not a loner weirdo, you know." His tone has cooled, and I feel like a jerk.

"I know. That's not what I meant, and I'm sorry."

He sighs, staring out the front windshield instead of at me. "You've heard what people say about my dad. If you think it'll spare me to lie and say you haven't, it won't."

I look at his profile; his face is emotionless, but his jaw is set with tension. "Yeah, I've heard."

He tears his gaze from the windshield, and his ice-blue eyes meet mine. "A lot of it's lies, of course, but I never . . . I think a lot of times people think I'm either to be pitied or else I'm just like him. They don't want to get to know me and figure out what I'm actually like."

"Well." I cautiously squeeze his hand. The car's got a dark energy now, like each word he spoke about his father spit poison into the air. My cast makes holding hands awkward, but when he looks down at my half-encased fingers clutching his, something relaxes in his expression. "It's their loss, Liam. If they don't want to get to know you as a person."

"Yeah?" He raises an eyebrow. "You know you were there, right? You didn't want to get to know me, either."

"Okay, but not because of *you*. I mean, I only had to talk to you like twice before I figured out Hunter was being insane."

He laughs. "I appreciate that. And I'm sorry, we were having a nice date and I made it uncomfortable."

"No." I shake my head and then regret it when the world spins for a second. "*I'm* the one who made it weird. You've been perfect."

As soon as I say it, I want to pull the words back down my throat because calling someone perfect on a first date is so incredibly dorky.

It seems to have been the right thing, though. A brilliant smile lights his face. He lets go of my cast-encased hand, traces the underside of my arm with his fingers, delicately, like my skin will crumble to dust if he presses too hard. Then he pulls my good hand to his face and kisses my wrist. I close my eyes, sighing shakily. He kisses farther up my forearm, his lips brushing my skin like eyelashes. The thrill of it sets my nerves on edge.

"Not getting any less perfect," I whisper.

One of his hands slides around my back, and his lips move to mine. I can hear myself breathing. I lean into him, but the cup holder stabs the edge of my knee like it's guarding him.

His hands move up my sides slowly like he's counting each of my ribs with his thumbs. My tongue grazes his lip. It tastes a little like chocolate. I realize his breathing is just as uneven as mine, and I try to press closer to him again.

The emergency brake stops me this time, knocking against my shin, reminding me that I'm in a car.

On a first date.

And maybe we shouldn't get carried away.

"Liam," I whisper. "Thank you for taking me to the Insectarium. Was it even fun for you?"

"Very, actually." He leans back against his seat, his chest rising and falling heavily. His hands leave my sides, but one slips down to rest on my leg for a moment before he twists the key, which sends his car rumbling to life. "I learned a lot about bugs."

"Is the educational element something you're usually looking for in a date?"

He laughs and glances at me as he pulls back onto the road. "I brought you there, Amelia. I wanted to go, and I'm glad we went."

His voice is so earnest, I can tell he means it, which is completely baffling to me. My insect hobby has always been something I do by myself. When Mom took me to the Insectarium, she politely pretended to care when I think in reality she was kind of dying inside. Liam doesn't even *like* insects, but he knows how much I do, and he's just . . . I twine my fingers around the hand he rests in my lap, unsure what to do with this heavy feeling of fondness that makes me want to wrap my arms around him and never let go.

Liam comes to a stop outside my house at 10:01, according to the faded green numbers on his dashboard. "I know you don't have to be home until eleven," he says, "but I want your parents to let me take you out again. Parents like boys who bring their daughters home early."

"Oh yeah? I like that you're an expert on what parents want you to do with their daughters."

He grins. "Just simple observations. Come on, I'll walk you to your door."

"Do parents like that, too?"

"I don't think parents have a preference one way or the other," he says. "But I'm pretty sure your brother would prefer I stay in the car."

I glance at the picture window in the living room. Mom's on the couch, facing away from us and reading a magazine. And, of course, Hunter and Sky are both pressed against the glass. Sky looks excited. Hunter, not so much.

"Your mom isn't watching, right?" Liam asks when we reach the door.

"Right," I confirm, glancing over his shoulder.

"Then . . . good night." He pulls me close and kisses me. A good, deep kiss. It would be better if I didn't think it was partly for the benefit of our little audience, though.

"I'll call you later this weekend, okay?" Liam says when he pulls away. I can't do anything except nod. I don't move until he's in his car, driving away. The kiss must've affected me more than I thought because I can only sort of feel my legs.

13

Sky and Hunter abandon me Monday morning when we arrive at school. They did this Friday, too, except I didn't care because I was so fixated on my date. Today, I kind of do care. I find Grace, Tera, and Roman hanging out near the arts building. Grace has straightened her hair and is wearing it in two loose braids. I tell myself that this is totally fine and normal and that seeing her wearing a completely new hairstyle that looks just as good as her regular hair doesn't make me feel anything inside. I yearn for the days when figuring out how I felt about Grace—and about girls—was my big focus. It was complicated, sure, but I didn't feel a specter of death looming over my shoulder like I do now. I'm so torn between *figure it out* and *let it go* that I'm frozen in a state of doing nothing and feeling like crap about it.

Liam, I remind myself. *He'll help you with this.*

"Let's hear it," says Tera the second I approach. "Since I basically match-made you, I deserve to hear all about your date."

"*You* match-made?" Roman interrupts.

"Yeah, obviously. I started dating you, then several months later, you told Amelia that Liam liked her, and now here we are."

"Oh, of course. How did I not put that together?" Roman laughs. Every time I hear male laughter now, I try to feel something from it, but the sensation of memory seems to be fickle. I wish that I understood more about memory and psychology and brains. I've done some reading online, but it's a different kind of science than I gravitate toward normally, and a lot of it is beyond me.

"It went well," I say. Out of habit, I reach to feel the smooth wood of the necklace that isn't there. I should get a new necklace so I can stop looking like a weirdo who strokes her clavicle. But I can't bring myself to. It's silly to be so in mourning about that necklace, but here we are.

"That is an extremely inadequate summary." Tera folds her arms and stares me down.

I don't want to talk about this in front of Grace. It makes me feel like I'm cheating on the crush I have on her, which is absolutely ridiculous. Her expression is neutral, and she's certainly been pushing me toward Liam as much as anyone else, so . . .

I give them a much more detailed story, ending with the part where Liam asked me to be his girlfriend when we talked on the phone last night. Tera practically swoons over this. She is a big romantic. And saying out loud that I have a boyfriend makes me feel kind of . . . well, *excited*, for the first time since my accident. My lingering aches and pains and fears all melt away and I'm just a girl with a new, hot boyfriend.

"How does Hunter feel about this?" Grace asks, and I deflate immediately.

"He's not thrilled. But I didn't see him much this weekend, so he can't be *that* displeased about it."

"Yeah, I mean, not his place to have an opinion anyway, right?" She inspects her nails, which are white with navy-blue French tips.

I wish I had any idea what was going on in her brain. Sometimes I feel like maybe she likes me, too, and then I figure I'm being delusional. She's my friend, and she cares about me. It doesn't mean she wants to kiss me. But if she *did* . . . Wow, I should not be thinking about this two seconds after I stopped being single.

"Not his place," I confirm. "Not at all."

Sky and Hunter go off together somewhere at lunch, too, and it puts me in a mood for the afternoon. It's not that I don't have other friends, it's just that Sky is my *best* friend and now that the secret's out about her relationship with Hunter, it seems like she's totally consumed by it. This wasn't something I considered when she first told me. I worried it would be weird (and gross) to watch her kiss my brother and that when I fought with either of them, I wouldn't be able to vent to the other anymore. I didn't think about how we've been a trio since we were kids and how this relationship between them might change our entire dynamic.

The team's in the state playoffs now, which means soccer

practices have amped up, which means I'm stuck waiting around even later for Hunter to be done, and Sky isn't here with me, because she has a dentist appointment. I finish all my homework, listen to two entomology podcasts, and read three articles about a new insect they discovered in Brazil. They really do not put an adequate amount of detail in these articles. I know most people don't care about receiving a full, in-depth account of the discovery, but some of us do. We are the ones they should be catering these articles to.

Restless, I pace the athletic building lobby and start thinking about Sky again. I get a little bit dizzy, and now I'm thinking about Sky *and* my accident. How she and Hunter fought here in this very building, how someone could have overheard them talking.

There's nothing better to do, so I head down the hall to the pool stairwell. I open the door at the top and listen to the echo it makes all the way down when I let it close heavily. It's a long flight of stairs with frequent turns and echoey walls, which makes it a popular spot for people to make out. If you're somewhere in the middle, it's practically impossible for anyone to catch you in the act.

I drum my fingernails against the metal stair railing. It's so loud. The door is thick and solid, but I still think if you were arguing loudly here at the top, someone outside it could probably hear you. I peek out the single narrow glass pane in an otherwise metal door, craning my neck to see how far my range of vision is. Someone could definitely hide just out of sight. And the boys are now headed down the hall to the locker room.

I wait for them all to go by before I emerge, because I don't need any pesky questions—like "why were you hanging out in the stairwell alone like a weirdo?"—and then I head back to the lobby and sit with my backpack until Liam appears.

"Hey," he says, and reaches for my hand.

"Hello."

Feeling bold, I kiss him, even though there are people around right now who will definitely have strong opinions about this. His disarming grin afterward makes me not care about anyone else's opinions.

"Waiting for Hunter to drive you home?" he asks.

"Yeah. As usual."

"You know, he's not the only one who could drive you home." He's holding both of my hands now. One normally, the other with his fingers looped around my cast as best as they can loop. I wish he was touching my skin instead of my bulky plaster nuisance.

"That's true. Are you offering?"

"No," says a voice behind him. Hunter, approaching with a scowl.

"Hunter." His name huffs out of my mouth in an annoyed sigh.

"Another time," Hunter says firmly, and I'm not going to argue with my brother here in the athletic building lobby.

"Fine." I look up at Liam. "I'll see you tomorrow?"

He nods and doesn't look too put out. I rise onto my toes, and he dips his head to kiss me. It's pretty chaste, but it still makes heat burn through me. Hunter has politely looked away, but he's scowling our whole walk back to the car. The weather has cooled, and I wish I'd worn a warmer jacket. Between the cold and the dark, I am deeply concerned that it might snow before the playoff finals on Friday. Fleetingly, I think it might be best if they don't make it to the finals, but then I feel bad. Hunter and Liam both deserve to go out with a win.

"Could you be, like, thirty percent less rude to him?" I ask as I plop into the passenger seat of the car. Hunter and I used to switch off which of us drove, and I miss it. The neurologist has instructed me not to drive again until I'm having *no* dizzy spells, and I'm starting to feel like that will never happen.

"I can do ten percent."

"It's not *funny*, Hunter. What would have been so bad about him driving me home?"

"I don't know. Nothing. He's just— You *know* I don't like him."

"Sure, but did you really think you would like everyone I ever dated?"

"Yes," he says sullenly, and then after I glare at him, he laughs. "I guess not. I'm sorry, Amelia. You just picked the one person I can't even *start* to get on board with."

"Why not, though? I mean, seriously? Because you guys

were middle school rivals and Liam kicked a soccer ball at your face in ninth grade? Come on, Hunter."

Hunter glances in my direction. "That's not why I don't like him. Do you really want to have this conversation?"

"I do, actually. You know his life hasn't been that easy, and you guys all ostracize him anyway."

"We don't ostracize him. He was invited to Alec's party and Alec doesn't even *like* him. Most of the other guys don't have any problem with him. His personality is fine, but he also gives off this air like he's better than the rest of us. It's not overt, it's just . . . an *air*. I don't know."

"So he has an air of superiority and that's why you two can never be friends?"

"*No*. I just . . . I don't know how to explain. We have a long and complicated history, and I don't trust him, and I want you to be careful, but I *will* try harder. I will be twenty percent nicer."

I roll my eyes, but he's being very earnest. "I'll take it."

"Good. Thank you."

"By the way, though, can you also please keep Sky from me, like, a little bit less?"

"Amelia," he says, exasperated. "I'm not keeping Sky from you. We're dating. I don't know if you know this, but people who are dating spend a lot of time together."

"Oh, do they? I wouldn't know. My brother wouldn't let my boyfriend drive me home from school."

He ignores that completely. "If you're not happy with how things are with Sky, you need to talk to her about it, not me. I'm just trying to, you know, make her happy."

"Okay. Got it." I don't want to talk to Sky because I can't tell if I'm being irrational. I want Hunter to realize on his own that he's taking her over. But I can see now that his priority is her, and it shouldn't hurt me, but it does. "Hunter?"

"Yeah?"

"If the soccer ball incident wasn't the thing that confirmed you and Liam never being friends, what was?"

He's quiet for a very long time. "There wasn't any one thing, Amelia. We just don't get along."

I don't know why he's doing it, but I know without a doubt that, once again, my brother is lying to me.

14

Over the next few days, I start to feel like myself again. Like a regular girl who just started dating a boy and has no nagging questions about what happened to her when she almost died. It's surprising how much more smoothly every single aspect of your life goes when you aren't fixating all your energy on something there's no way you could ever solve.

My concerns aren't *gone*; they're still lurking in the background, waiting for me to let my guard down so they can emerge. Like right now, as I sit in the bleachers, watching the soccer team warm up before their final playoff game.

Should I be thinking more about this? Should I be trying to deal with whatever happened to me so it doesn't happen again to others? I'm finding myself reaching a whole lot of dead ends, and I'm not confident in my Suspicious People list. It's so short and based on so little evidence. The only person on it who gives me a real creep vibe is Mr. Omerton, and he gives me *such* a creep vibe that I don't want to be anywhere near him. Which means I don't know how to rule him out. And there's Liam's dad, based on nothing except the fact that I still haven't met him and Liam practically develops a storm cloud over his head when he mentions him. And Clarissa, who's done nothing really to earn her place but who I can't quite cross off, even though my gut feeling is that whoever did this to me was male.

I haven't remembered anything new from that day, and my neurologist says it's extremely unlikely that I ever will. I told her about what happens sometimes when I hear laughter, and she seemed to think it was just a coping mechanism for my brain. I want to remember something so badly that I'm making it up, basically. But there's still that feeling of someone pushing me, too. And my necklace snapping loose. She's probably right. She certainly has a much better understanding of how brains work and how they process trauma. It just all feels so *real*, it's hard to let go of.

Sky returns from the vending machine in the athletic building, and she's picked up Grace on the way. I'm relieved to see them, because being alone with my thoughts doesn't seem to be working for me.

The stands fill up quickly as the game time approaches. If we win tonight, we'll be state champions for the third year in a row. Fans of both teams are tense, and the players are, too. Hunter has his Serious Frown and Liam's shoulders look like they're being lifted by puppet strings.

The game is close and stressful; I can't stop cleaning my glasses on my shirt as though one speck of dust might prevent me from seeing all the action. Sky's bitten her nails to stubs. Grace doesn't care so much about soccer as she does about hanging out with us, but even she sits unmoving except for intermittent hisses of breath when something bad happens.

Sometime during the fourth quarter, I have to pee badly enough that the porta potty on the edge of the field finally starts to look acceptable. I regret it the moment I enter the overwarm box of sewage and upsettingly moist air. And as much as I love spiders, the number in here disturbs me slightly.

On my way back to the bleachers, I stop short. Clarissa has broken away from a cluster of her friends, and she's headed this way. I've been wanting to get her alone for weeks, to talk to her and convince myself that she doesn't belong on my list.

"Good luck," I say when she passes me. "It's gross in there."

She gives me the same look of disgust that I gave the porta potty, and it makes me furious.

"Hey, what is your problem, exactly?" I turn to face her, arms folded tight. "You've never liked me, and I've never done anything to you."

"Oh, you haven't?" Her eyes flash with genuine anger. It surprises me. "You think I don't know that you told your brother he should dump me from day one? Must be pretty happy now that you've got him dating the exact person you want him to."

Her gaze flicks to the bleachers in the distance, and I know she's looking at Sky. As though having my best friend become more interested in my brother than she is in me is exactly what I needed right now.

"Hunter's dating life is none of my business. I certainly never told him how he should or shouldn't feel about you. But *you* didn't like when he spent time with me, which is pretty ridiculous, you know. If your boyfriend's going to hang out with another girl, isn't it ideal that the girl he's hanging out with is *his sister*?"

"Whatever. There's nothing great or special about you, Amelia, but I guess if you can leverage clumsiness into attention from guys way out of your league like Liam, good for you."

She's *jealous*, I realize, completely taken aback. Clarissa is beautiful and popular, but she wants people to notice her the way they've noticed me ever since my accident.

"Liam's not out of her league," says a voice behind me. Grace. "What is your problem, Clarissa?"

"Man stealers are my problem," Clarissa snarls. "Get out of my face, both of you."

And she walks away. I'm totally bewildered.

"She wasn't dating Liam, was she?" I ask, starting back toward the bleachers.

Grace shrugs. "Not that I know of? Maybe she just wanted to. Are you okay?"

"I'm fine. I initiated the conversation, so I can't really be upset about the outcome."

But I am upset, actually. It hurts to have someone dislike you the way Clarissa clearly dislikes me. I don't do anything to set myself up for hatred like that, and it feels *bad*. I'm as gossipy as the next person, and there are people I just don't like for whatever reason, but to make it so obvious *to their face* when there's no merit for your dislike? It's cruel.

"I don't know what I did to her."

Grace looks at me with sympathy. "You didn't do anything. Whatever her problem is with you, it's . . . well, *her problem*. You're great, okay? I know you don't need me to tell you that, but you are."

"So are you," I tell her, with a sad smile.

We're nearly back to our seats, but she stops me with a hand on my arm. Her mouth opens and closes, but she says nothing. Instead, she hugs me tight. Sometimes a gesture says more than words can, and hers reminds me that it doesn't matter what Clarissa thinks about me, because I have friends who think I'm worth a whole lot, and that's what matters.

A screaming cheer rises from the stands. I turn toward the field just in time to see the game end, and with our team winning by one goal.

"What happened?" I ask.

Grace shakes her head. "I didn't see. But it looks like . . . maybe Liam scored a goal?"

Based on the way the rest of the team is piling all over him, I think she's right. My heart sinks. I should not have missed this important moment, even if I didn't miss it on purpose. Liam has no one else here to watch him.

And the whole time his teammates are cheering and tackling him, he's staring straight at me.

I find Liam after everyone's gotten settled down postgame. As usual, he says no to coming to dinner with my family, not that I expected any different. Even when he comes to my house, he doesn't seem entirely comfortable with meals where the whole family gathers. I can only assume it's to do with the fact that his father barely participates in his life, but anytime we remotely circle the topic of his home life, he changes the subject.

My parents take Hunter to the restaurant in their car, with Sky and me promising to follow in a few minutes in ours. Sky walks Grace back to her dorm, giving me a little bit of time with Liam. He and I sit on the hood of my car in the nearly empty school parking lot. Some dorm students are playing Frisbee by the light of the streetlamps in the lower lot, and they're taking it much more seriously than I ever would.

"I'm sorry I missed your last goal," I say. I've already said it, and he's already forgiven me, but I feel guilty about it still.

"Amelia." My name is a sigh. "You've seen nearly every goal I've made in my life. Don't worry about it. You couldn't have known Grace was going to distract you at the exact moment I scored."

Our hands are intertwined. I squeeze his. "I'll make it up to you somehow."

"Yeah?" He grins. "I look forward to that."

"You should." I slip down off the hood of my car, pull him with me so that we never really stop being wrapped up in each other. "Are you *sure* you don't want to come to dinner with us?"

I ask him the question and then I kiss him so he can't answer right away.

It doesn't work. "I'm sure," he says, but he doesn't really stop kissing me to say it.

"Fine," I sigh. "But I'm proud of you and *eventually*, I'm going to get you to celebrate your achievements."

He laughs. "Stranger things have happened, I'm sure."

Sky approaches, her footsteps echoing against the pavement. I look up at Liam and smile. "Last chance," I tell him.

His smile is broad as he kisses me one more time. "Good try."

Sky gets into the driver's seat, so I reluctantly leave Liam's side.

"Couldn't get him to come with us, huh?" Sky says, backing slowly out of the parking spot.

"No." I frown. I want to enjoy the time I have right now with Sky, be fully here and in the moment. We don't have these times as much anymore and I miss it. But I'm still thinking about Liam and guilty I missed his goal, and I kind of hate leaving him here. Alone in the parking lot. Always alone. He won the game tonight and this is all he gets.

It doesn't seem fair.

15

One of my favorite November traditions is the Maple Hill craft fair at the town hall. Usually I go with Mom and Sky, but today Sky has plans with Hunter instead.

"It's his first day of freedom," she told me this morning when I called about what time she would come over. "No more soccer unless he plays in college."

I feigned nonchalance about this because it embarrassed me that I hadn't considered this scenario. This is *tradition*. I thought that meant you got to assume.

But when I texted Grace, a little poutingly, to see what *she* was up to today, she coerced Tera into borrowing her mom's car and driving out. Now the three of us and my mom are all at the town hall, which greets us with the scent of doughnuts and other baked goods. The upstairs of the building is a basketball court, usually lined with bleachers, though those have been taken out for today's festivities. There's a stage at the back where kids from the elementary school (including me, when I was younger) perform concerts and plays. This is also where people come to vote on election days. Downstairs there are bathrooms, a kitchen, and a big area filled with tables, which gets used for a lot of functions. The craft fair has taken over both upstairs and down. People with tables are selling jams and wood-carved items and honey and soap and hand towels and pot holders and mail-boxes and all manner of things.

"This is wild," Grace says approvingly. "I won't even be able to describe this to my parents."

The three of us take a selfie near the door, getting thoroughly in the way of anyone who wants to pass by.

"Girls," says Mom in her exasperated tone. "Get out of everyone's way, and I will take a picture for you. It's so much easier."

I give her my phone, and the three of us pose together while she snaps pictures.

"Ooh, Amelia," she says, phone still raised. "You're getting texts from a *boy*."

She knows exactly which boy it is, but she also loves embarrassing me. "Oh my God, Mom, give it back."

As I assumed, it's Liam, asking what I'm up to today.

At the craft fair with my mom & grace & tera, I text back.

Not Sky?

That hits me in a sore spot, so all I say is, No.

"I want this," says Grace. She's running her fingers over a towel with a cute reindeer and a knitted loop at the top with a button so you can hang it from your stove.

"Get it! They're like two dollars usually." I join her at the display. There are always tons of these, and they're always very cute.

"And where, exactly, do I put this in my dorm room?"

"Hang it from your doorknob," Tera suggests.

"You know what, that's kind of brilliant." Grace hands the vendor her cash, and we move along. While Grace and Tera look at some hand-knitted mittens, I stop by the booth where they make bowls and other decorative items out of wood scraps. They're so expensive but so beautiful, and they make me think of my necklace. It might not be as complex as these giant bowls, but I loved it so much and I loved that Dad and Hunter made it together and I just . . . want it back.

"Hey," says a voice at my ear. I turn, and Liam's standing there.

"Oh, hey." It doesn't sound enthusiastic enough, but I wasn't expecting to see him here.

He dips his head and kisses me, and again, I'm not expecting it so I just stand there like a lifeless blob of flesh. He pulls away.

"Should I not have done that here?" he asks, frowning, and I feel the curious eyes of my friends upon us.

"No, I— Of course you should. I just totally didn't expect to see you here." I smile at him warmly and take his hand. "But I'm glad."

It isn't a lie, but it kind of feels like one. I'm glad to see him and his disarming smile, but I also feel weird because I'm a little mad at Sky for abandoning me in favor of Hunter, and now suddenly my boyfriend's here pulling my attention away from the friends who actually had time for me today.

"What're you interested in here?" Liam asks, gesturing to the table of wooden decorative items.

"Oh, it's all too expensive. Beautiful though, right? I was just thinking about the necklace I lost when I had my accident." I clutch at the nothing around my neck again. "I miss it."

"I remember that necklace," he says, tracing my throat with a fingertip. "I'm sorry you lost it."

"Me too. It meant a lot to me. It's stupid."

He doesn't say anything, but he looks sympathetic. I mean, what is he supposed to say, really.

"Hey Amelia, what do you think?" Grace interrupts, modeling a knitted hat. Behind her, Tera holds up hands encased in mittens that have bells sewn into the backs.

"Well, the hat is great, but the mittens are a must-have," I say, laughing.

"Totally agree," says Tera, and she does actually buy them. "By the way," she adds, close to my ear, "Liam's definitely here because he's jealous of Grace."

"You're ridiculous," I tell her, but she rolls her eyes and tugs me away. "We'll be right back, going to the bathroom," I say to Grace.

Downstairs, when we're closed behind the heavy wooden door of the ladies bathroom, Tera peers under the stall doors for feet and then says, "It's not a bad thing for him to have a little new-boyfriend jealousy, you know."

"Yeah, but why of Grace?" My stomach is in knots because I love Tera, but I don't need her to know about my crush.

"Because Grace is beautiful, and Grace always looks at you like she wants to kiss you."

I scoff. "She does not."

Tera looks nervous. "Don't tell her I said that, okay? She'd kill me. But yeah, she absolutely does."

I don't know what to say to that, so what I say is, "I actually kind of *do* have to go to the bathroom," and close myself into a stall.

If Grace actually *did* like me, I don't know what I'd do. But I think Tera's wrong about this. She tends to see romance in places where it doesn't exist, and there's no way Grace could possibly be interested in me.

But I think Tera *is* right that Liam's feeling a little jealous. And if I'm being completely honest, I like it.

16

When we're done at the craft fair, Grace and Tera head back to St. Elm, and Liam comes over to my house. By some miracle of miracles, he agrees to stay for dinner. This may be largely thanks to my dad, who insists. Well, *demands*, more like. My parents are both majorly bossy people, and my dad wants to get to know Liam better if he's going to be a fixture in our lives, which, of course, I hope he is. So Dad is going to get to know him whether Liam likes it or not.

Dinner is a roast Mom made in the Crock-Pot and it's delicious. Dad spends the whole meal asking Liam a million questions about himself and dishing out some unnecessary but very dad-like teasing about Maple Hill's superiority over Hen Falls. Liam takes it all in stride, which is a relief because if I were him, I would be thoroughly unamused by this grill session. He doesn't seem upset, though. He almost seems to enjoy being included in my family like this.

"When am I going to meet *your* dad?" I ask Liam when we

wander outside afterward, just the two of us. It's chilly out after dark, and I'm wearing a puffy jacket, but he doesn't seem too cold in just a St. Elm soccer hoodie.

"Oh, eventually," he says with a wry smile. "But I'm warning you now, you'll wish you hadn't."

"I'm sure it won't be as bad as you think."

He shrugs, and it isn't an irritated gesture, but I can tell he doesn't want to talk about this anymore. I take his hand, and we just walk. Alone in the peace and quiet of the evening.

Our yard is quite large, but a lot of it is taken up by Dad's garage, which can fit two trucks inside it, plus all his tools and filters and parts and supplies. After we're done circling, we start up the road a little bit.

"Are you and Sky fighting?" he asks.

"No." I push my glasses higher on my nose. "Why do you ask?"

"You told me yesterday she always goes to the craft fair with you."

"Oh. Yeah. She decided to hang out with Hunter instead. It's fine. It's what happens, you know? New boyfriends change things, and we'll adjust." I don't want Liam to know how much it bothers me, because he's *my* new boyfriend, and we already started things out by talking about my problems—bonding over the suspicious nature of my accident. That's already a thing that's taking up so much of my mental energy that I don't need to also complain to him about feeling abandoned in favor of my brother by my best friend. Liam will get tired of me so fast if all I do is complain about my entire life.

"But she's your best friend," he says. "She shouldn't abandon you like that."

"I guess not."

"You don't really want to talk about it, huh?"

I shake my head.

He lets go of my hand and winds his arm around my waist instead. "Well, I'm here for you. When you do want to."

I smile up at him. "You are good at that, aren't you?"

His eyes glint with an indefinable emotion in the fading light of dusk. "With you I am."

We walk in silence for a couple of minutes, which I find peaceful but Liam seems to find uncomfortable.

"You must be ready to have that cast off," he says. "Tuesday, right?"

"Yep." I glance down at the stupid, itchy thing. "And then everyone can stop asking me about it all the time."

"Including me."

I laugh. "I don't mind it so much when you ask. You don't ask me like you think I'm going to break, but more like . . . you're curious about the healing process."

"That's pretty accurate. I mean, don't *you* find the process interesting? You got so lucky, and all the reminders that something happened to you are slowly healing themselves away."

"That's an interesting way to view healing." I pause to think about it for a few seconds. "I think I like it."

We're almost back to my house, and my heart sinks because Mr. Omerton is on his front porch, calling us over.

"Who's that?" Liam asks quietly.

"Creepy neighbor," I mutter. "Let's just go over there real quick."

We stand on his front porch, not near him.

"Hi, Mr. Omerton," I say politely. "You need something?"

"No, just sitting out here and saw you walk by." He's swaying gently on a porch swing, and I don't know why but it gives me a full-body shudder of disgust. "You don't seem to notice me usually, when you're out jogging."

"Oh, I don't? I'm always wearing headphones, so I'm pretty oblivious to my surroundings, I guess."

"Doesn't seem like a great idea, to be oblivious," he says.

"No, probably not. Anyway, my boyfriend and I need to get back inside; it was nice talking with you."

I don't introduce Liam because like hell am I going to give this man any information about my life.

"You too, Amelia. Try to pay more attention when you're jogging, would you? Smile at me every now and then."

I don't say anything in response, just keep my face arranged very definitely not in a smile and drag Liam away.

"That was . . . odd," Liam says once we're out of earshot.

"That's one word to describe it. Don't look back. Spoiler alert: He'll still be watching."

Liam frowns. "Is that guy on your list of suspicious people? If not, he should be."

"Oh yeah. He's at the top."

"Good. Well, not *good*, but you know what I mean."

We're on my porch now, and I risk a casual glance in Mr. Omerton's direction. Still watching, as predicted.

"Yeah," I say, zipping my coat tighter to my chin. "I do."

17

Tuesday is the long-awaited day: my cast removal. Mom picks me up from school and brings me to the hospital, and Aunt Jenna comes, too, so she can decode anything the doctor says that we don't understand. I'm so excited, I can't hold still in the waiting room, which makes Aunt Jenna laugh.

"You're acting like a ten-year-old," she says.

"Have *you* ever had a cast? This thing weighs thirty pounds; I'm beyond ready to be rid of it."

"Thirty pounds? That seems excessive. We should talk to someone about that."

I roll my eyes at her, and she laughs again, but fortunately I'm called in before she can tease me more. After a last X-ray to make sure my arm looks good, the doctor removes the cast. My arm is disgusting. There's no sugarcoating it. My skin is flaky and pale and smelly. It doesn't really hurt, but my muscles are weak and bending my wrist takes a lot of effort. The doctor wants to refer me to a physical therapist, but Aunt Jenna promises she'll work with me.

"You're already seeing enough doctors," she says as the three of us leave the hospital. "No sense sending you to a PT when your aunt is one and can do it at home for free."

"And will do a better job than whoever he was going to refer her to, anyway," Mom adds.

I'm too busy appraising my wrist to care about any of this right now. I'm relieved when we get home and I get the thing cleaned up so I don't smell like old cheese anymore, but my skin is sensitive, and I hate that I can't bend my wrist the whole way yet and that even without my cast I still feel delicate and damaged. Back in my room, I text a picture of my freed arm to all my friends. The responses range from wow, so you CAN be whiter (Roman) to lookin good (Grace) to can I come see that liberated arm after school? (Liam).

I text of course to Liam and then wait impatiently in the living room for everyone to get home. Hunter and Sky arrive first, and I hold out my arm like it's a totally new limb no one's ever seen before.

"It looks skinny," says Hunter.

"It looks *great*," says Sky.

"It's looked better," I admit. "But it'll come back to life now that it's, like, exposed to oxygen again."

"I'm happy for you." Sky hugs me. "I know that cast really sucked."

"Yeah, I hope I never have to have one again." Now if I can just get my brain to stop having its occasional headaches and dizzy spells, everything can go back to normal.

Normal-ish. "And I would recommend neither of *you* ever get one, either."

"Noted," says Hunter.

"What are you doing now?" Sky asks. "Want to hang out with us?"

"Liam's coming over, but we could all—"

"No," Hunter interrupts immediately. "I am not hanging out with Liam."

"Seriously? You can't be pleasant to him for my sake even for one afternoon?"

"Nope."

Sky rolls her eyes but doesn't step in.

"Okay, well, I guess I'll see you guys whenever, then."

I turn away from them both and go out on the porch to wait for Liam. Sky never comes out to apologize or to see if I'm okay or anything, so I'm fuming by the time he pulls in, but I don't want him to know that. I siphon my rage energy into trotting over to his car and greeting him the moment he steps out.

"Nice arm," he says, running his fingertips over my skin.

"I'll keep it." I grin, and then kiss him. "Come on, let's go in my dad's shop. I'm annoyed at Hunter and I don't want to be near him."

He doesn't protest, though I'm sure my dad's shop is not his ideal environment. The shop has bays for two trucks, the floor is stained with oil spots, and the whole thing has a hint of diesel smell that never dissipates.

"What do you think?" I ask.

"I think . . . I won't touch any of the walls."

I laugh. "It's not actually that filthy, you know, it's just . . . it's a shop."

He walks slowly through it, eyeing some of the tools and barrels of oil and my dad's neatly organized array of filters and greases and windshield fluid. "Never really thought about how much it takes to keep one of those things running."

"Yeah, they put on a lot of miles compared to, like, a regular vehicle, and they're dragging heavy trailers behind them, so it's a lot of wear and tear. Seems like one of Dad's trucks is broken about every single week. He loves having a trucking company, though, so I guess that's good?"

"Always important, I think. My dad always hated his jobs. Even working from home didn't seem to make him any happier. And working from home means he never has to talk to people, which is his ideal. Especially with how people think of him around here."

"Is . . . it *wrong*, how people think of him?" I ask hesitantly. Liam's so closed off about discussing his family, but he brought it up. He seems defensive of his father, while simultaneously . . . hating him? I can't figure it out.

Liam shrugs. "People always think they have such a good read on situations, but they really don't know anything. My dad's not great; I don't think you'd believe me if I said he was. But my mom wasn't exactly innocent. I'm glad she's been gone so long. She was . . ." He trails off and looks at me with fire in his eyes. "I don't want to talk about it anymore."

"Okay. What *do* you want to talk about?"

Nothing is the answer, but he doesn't say it aloud. He says it by cupping my face in his hands and kissing me. Kissing me with force. I wrap both arms around his neck, happy I can do this now without risk of knocking him out with my cast. His hands move to my waist, holding me close. He kisses me so hard I can barely breathe. I feel *wanted*, and I like that feeling. It chases all the other things away. The fear and the pain and the creeping worry that Sky will start liking Hunter more than she likes me. I brush my recently uncasted hand along Liam's cheek, enjoying the feeling of skin on my long-deprived skin.

He reaches for my hand, runs his fingers down my wrist. Presses his lips to my pulse.

"Have you done anything about that man yet?" he asks. "Your creepy neighbor?"

I shake my head. He and I have barely talked about solving the mystery of my accident since we started dating, and he wants to talk about it *now*?

"I can help you," he whispers, his lips grazing my earlobe. "I can help you figure out how to get him to stop staring at you so much."

"Please do." I hold very still, closing my eyes and tilting my head while his lips trail down the side of my neck.

"No one should stare at you as much as he does." Liam's hand slides down my arm, back to my newly freed wrist, which he grips loosely. "No one except me."

I smile, and he kisses me again. His grip tightens on my wrist, which protests.

"Liam," I mumble against his mouth. "That hurts."

"Does it?" He loosens his grip, pulls away, and holds up my arm. "I thought it was supposed to be healed?"

"Well, yeah, the bone is, but it hasn't been exposed to the elements in a while. The muscles are a little atrophied and stuff."

"Oh." He rotates my hand slowly, watches me grimace when he hits its limits. Then he holds it to his mouth. "I'll be gentle."

"Starting when?" I ask as he presses his fingertips into the sides of my wrist, eliciting another pain response, which I'm sure shows in my face.

"Now," he says, and drops my wrist.

We stay in the truck shop for another half hour. And he does keep his word.

U around?

This text from Grace interrupts me in the middle of a YouTube video I'm watching about bullet ants later that night.

Yes why??

And then my phone rings.

"I think someone's . . . watching me," she says, without preamble.

"What do you mean, watching you?"

"Like, I don't know. Maybe I'm being crazy, but there have been several times over the past couple of days when I felt that, like, skin-crawling sensation where there are eyes on me. Do you know what I'm talking about?"

"All too well, unfortunately."

"Do you think I'm being paranoid?" There's desperation in her voice. She wants me to say yes, but . . .

"No. I don't."

Silence.

"Grace?"

"I'm just . . . processing. It's connected to you, isn't it?" The unspoken actual question: *It's because someone knows how you feel about me, isn't it?* "Your fall was no accident, right?"

I move my glasses, folded on my nightstand, in a slow circle. "I can't tell you that for sure, but . . . it'd be my guess."

Again, silence.

"Grace, if you want to distance yourself from me for a little while, I would completely understand, and I—"

"No," she says stubbornly. "Absolutely not."

"But, Grace, if I'm—"

"Look, I don't think I'm in *danger*, exactly," she says, even though she obviously wouldn't be calling me to talk about this if she didn't think that was a possibility. "Someone could be watching me for a lot of reasons, or no one could actually be watching me at all. I just have to be careful for now, until I figure it out. Please don't be worried, and please don't feel guilty."

"I'm *going* to worry about you. I didn't want— You shouldn't be involved in this at all."

"I shouldn't? Well, neither should you," she says.

I can't argue with that, but I need to say *something*. "I'm going to figure out who might have tried to hurt me, okay? I *will* figure it out."

"I know you will."

I can hear it in her voice, that she really does believe in me. But instead of making me feel buoyed, it makes me feel burdened. If I don't figure this out, I'm letting her down. Or worse.

After we hang up, I pull out my laptop and open up a search engine. I told Liam that Mr. Omerton was at the top of my list, and I didn't really think about how true that is. He's the most obviously suspicious person in my life. He used to just be an average parent-aged single guy, but he's gotten so *weird* lately. Staring at me all the time, telling me to smile, trying to lure me over to his house. And what do I even know about him, beyond surface things?

I search his name and come up totally empty. No social media profiles, no articles, no anything. Strange. He's too young to be so off the grid. If he were in his fifties or sixties, maybe. But it's uncommon for someone his age to have absolutely no online footprint. I pull up Maple Hill's town page on Facebook and scroll through recent event pictures until I find one that he's in. I crop the picture to remove extraneous faces, and then drop it into the search engine.

Nothing.

How has he stayed so anonymous? And more importantly, *why*?

I'm frustrated that once again, I've come up completely empty on information. How am I ever supposed to figure this out when nothing at all goes my way?

I slam the laptop shut and move to my window. His car's not there, and all his lights are off. I know he was home earlier, because Liam and I saw him when we left the truck shop. But it's been hours since then. He could have gone grocery shopping, or he could be at work. I have no way of knowing when he might be back.

But I feel reckless. My wrist is itchy and sore, I'm getting a headache, and I'm furious that someone is frightening Grace. It's only nine thirty, so Mom's still downstairs and Hunter's playing Fortnite in his room. It's impossible to creep past Mom with our house's layout, so I tell her I heard that a rare type of locust changed its migration pattern and they only travel at night, and that I want to go see if there might be any in our field.

She knows nothing about insects, so she accepts this easily even though it's freezing out and just tells me to make sure I use a flashlight.

I do use a flashlight, till I get near the road, where I switch it off. If Mr. Omerton comes home while I'm snooping, I don't need a giant beacon announcing my presence.

Also, I don't know what I'm doing. I can't break into his house because not only is that illegal but also I don't have the skills and don't even know exactly what skills I would need. He lived somewhere larger than Maple Hill before he moved here, and he definitely is not the type to leave his doors unlocked.

His garage, however, *is* unlocked. It's not attached to his house, and there's a door near the back that allows me to slip inside. I hold up my phone, letting the light from my screen illuminate the darkness a little bit. Nothing to see here, really. It's packed with things like a lawn mower and a snowblower and multiple chest freezers and a bunch of Christmas decorations—he goes all out on the Christmas decorations. I now understand why he parks his car outside. There's absolutely no room in here.

I pull my jacket sleeve over my hand and lift the lid on one of the freezers. Deer meat, mostly. I look in the other chest freezers, too, and find frozen veggies and pizzas and things like that. Nothing sinister. I don't know what I expected or what I would even have done if I'd found a chopped-up body, but thinking about that reminds me that I am snooping around my next-door neighbor's and that I should not linger. Carefully, I shut the door of the garage and sneak around the back of his house. I have to turn my phone's flashlight back on to see anything, because every single light in his house is off. I look in each window I can get to, and nothing seems out of the ordinary, until I come to a room that looks like an office. A laptop sitting on a desk with papers stacked around it. And there's a picture peeking out from the stack of papers. It's a school picture, I can tell by the background, even though it's only the bottom couple of inches.

It's *my* school picture, from last year. I was wearing a light blue shirt and, as always, my necklace.

I jump back from the window and hurry to my house,

beyond creeped out. What is he doing with a picture of me? How did he get it and *why* and—I think I have to tell my parents now about his creepy behavior, but I have to figure out a way to do it and have them take me seriously without admitting I went over there tonight and snooped around, because they will not approve of that.

Back in my room, I peer out my window. His car pulls in; I left just in time.

I reach up to pull down my shade but as I do, I swear, he is once again looking directly at me.

18

I've started to become kind of obsessed with Calvin Omerton. All the things I know about him (not many things) keep running through my head—and all the things I *don't* know, too. I need more information, so much more, and I don't have the means to collect the information. I should tell Mom. I *have* to tell Mom.

He basically *is* my Suspicious People list now. I mean, he certainly doesn't have my school picture just for the fun of it. I will tell Mom after school today, whether or not that means I have to admit to snooping over there. It's too important to keep to myself.

"Amelia?"

I'm totally caught. Liam obviously asked me something, but I was so not listening.

"Sorry . . . what?"

He laughs, pushing my math book out of the way so he can sit closer to me on the couch in the school library. "I said, we should have dinner out on Friday. At six?"

"Sounds awesome."

"Okay, good." He pulls out his beloved thick, leather-bound planner from his backpack and starts scribbling.

"Are you . . . writing that down?"

His pen stops moving, and I swear he pulls his leather monstrosity closer like he's protecting it from me. "Uh, yeah. Why?"

"No reason."

He glances suspiciously at me, then snatches my planner—thin and flimsy, school-provided—from where it peeks out of my open backpack.

"Hey!" I protest when he starts skimming through it.

"This is *empty*. How do you know when assignments are due? When you have tests? When games are?"

"I just . . . remember? We always have those papers that tell us when tests are . . ." I rummage through the mess of papers in my bag, holding up the first one I find that proves my point.

He just stares. "Give me that. And find me the rest of them."

I hand it over with more than a little trepidation and watch as he spends the next ten minutes writing down all my assignments and tests. And not only that but little blocks of time on Saturday mornings that he labels "hanging out with Liam," and also our Friday date.

"What if I don't want to hang out with you every Saturday?" I joke, feeling scarily organized. "What if I want to hang out with Hunter instead?"

"Go for it." He frowns, looking a little hurt.

"Oh, come on. I'm just teasing you." I lean over and kiss him on the cheek. "I think it's cute."

He nods, still looking sullen. And now I feel bad.

"It really will help me to have all this written down." I take my planner and shove it into my backpack. "I think sometimes—"

We're interrupted by the librarian, who bustles over with a serious expression on her face. We're not doing anything wrong—we aren't even touching at the moment—so her expression makes me very nervous.

"The headmaster has just called an emergency school assembly," the librarian says. "So you'll want to head over there right away."

I can't speak, but Liam thanks her. An emergency assembly is never good. I have the horrible feeling it means someone else has died.

"You okay?" Liam asks as we step outside of the library. "You look pale."

I slip my hand into his as we walk. "No, I'm fine. Just anxious to hear what this is about."

The assembly hall is a square building with seating leading up to a stage at the front and more seating in an upper level at the back. It doubles as a theater for plays and other performances. For our daily morning assemblies, we have assigned seats, but when we arrive it's all chaos, so Liam and I sit together near the side exit that connects to the math building.

Liam doesn't stop holding my hand even though my fingers are sweaty. He doesn't stop holding my hand the entire way through the emergency assembly. While the headmaster stands next to a state cop and tells us that a student went missing last night. While he tells us that her body was found today after a thorough search of the Connecticut River, on the Vermont side of the Comerford Dam, and that foul play is suspected. While he tells us that it was Lydia Kormel, Alec's sister. While he tells us that we are having this assembly because there have been *other incidents* that are now considered possibly suspicious as well. While he asks us to be understanding and respectful of the family during their time of loss.

By the time it's over, I feel dizzy and sick, and I realize I've dug crescents into Liam's hand with my nails. He leads me out, down the hallway through the math building and into the closed stairwell on the other side.

"Are you all right?" he asks, and immediately I burst into tears.

He wraps his arms around me, and I sob helplessly into his chest, frightened and unashamed. Am I one of the *other incidents*? Or is he only referring to Maria? I'm relieved—kind of—that something's suspicious this time, but I'm terrified by the implications, and horribly, horribly sad that this has happened again.

"You're kind of scaring me, Amelia," he says, but he holds me tight and it's what I need.

"I feel . . . I'm so afraid that they—whoever they are—that they'll come back for me." I sit heavily on the bottom step of the stairwell and pull off my glasses to wipe my eyes. "And I want to know . . . *why*? What did I do that would make someone want to hurt me?"

"Maybe it's nothing to do with you at all." Liam sits beside me, slings an arm around my shoulders. I wonder if this new death makes this all too real for him. "You can't know why a person would do something like that. Maybe you were just in the wrong place at the wrong time."

"I don't want to have been. I don't want any of this to have happened. This could have been *my* family grieving. They don't deserve this. Lydia's family doesn't deserve this."

A door opens, and someone starts down the stairwell. I try to look less upset, shove my glasses back on to hide my red, puffy eyes.

But it doesn't matter, because it's Hunter.

He takes us both in, then sits on the other side of me. "I was looking for you. Can we talk alone for a sec?"

"Sure." I squeeze Liam's hand.

"I should stay," he says. "You're too upset. I don't want to leave you."

"Are you trying to imply something, Liam?" Hunter snaps, eyes narrowed.

"Hunter, don't," I intercede. "Liam, please just give us a minute."

I can tell he doesn't want to. He hesitates for a long time, frowning at my brother. But he relents.

"I'll be just outside," he says.

Hunter rolls his eyes.

"I'm going to take you home," he says as soon as the door's closed. "I called Mom and told her everything's fine but we need to talk to her. I hope that's okay. This has just—I know you didn't want to talk about this with her or Dad, but I think we need to now. I think there've been too many similar incidents, and now apparently things are officially suspicious, and maybe it's time to get their advice on whether there's something we should do to protect you? I mean . . . I don't know, Amelia, what do you think?"

"I think . . ." I sigh, shakily. "You're right. It's time to tell Mom. I was feeling like I wanted to talk to her anyway. But don't you think it can wait till the end of the school day?"

"No, we should go home now. This is too important, and I don't even like the thought of you walking around school like normal for the rest of the day. I know that's overprotective, and I'm sorry, but that's how I feel. You've already been hurt, and I thought—" His voice catches and he swallows hard. "I'm not going to be the guy who loses his sister. I'm just not."

"Okay," I say softly. "Okay, we'll go now. We'll go talk to Mom."

It scares me to imagine talking about this with an adult. Scares me because it makes it *real*. It turns this into more than me trying desperately to believe that something less embarrassing happened to me than an accidental fall. This isn't the kind of less-embarrassing I want. It's the kind of less-embarrassing that keeps you awake at night, that slithers into your darkest dreams. But I want to be safe and I'm so afraid. Afraid that staying away from rivers isn't good enough. That whoever's doing this will be back for me.

And I don't want Hunter to be the guy who loses his sister, either.

Mom's sitting on the couch when we get home, scrolling on her phone. When she sees us, she shuts off her screen and moves to the kitchen. She gestures for us to sit at the island.

"Should I prepare myself to be mad? I couldn't tell from Hunter's call."

"No," I say quickly. "We didn't do anything. It's just—"

I look to Hunter, who nods and smiles encouragingly.

"Another girl died—Lydia Kormel, her brother's on Hunter's soccer team. They found her body in the Connecticut, and the headmaster said that foul play is suspected, and that now there are other incidents considered suspicious." I take a deep breath before continuing. It's one thing conjecturing to my brother and Liam and Sky and Grace. It's something else entirely to tell my mom. What if she doesn't believe me? What if she thinks I'm just projecting? "That's the third girl in two months, Mom."

"Counting you." Her words are steady, but she presses her phone tight between her hands.

"Counting me. I feel . . . scared."

Mom comes around the island and wraps her arms around me. "I don't blame you."

"Mom, what do you think?" Hunter asks, his brow furrowed.

Mom sighs and kisses my hair. "The police have probably already made the connection at this point, but I'll give them a call. To be honest, I considered this fleetingly after I heard about poor Maria, but I thought I was just being a paranoid mother. But now . . . I don't want to scare you, Amelia, but I think maybe when you—"

She cuts herself off abruptly and hugs me tight again. I want to tell her that it doesn't scare me more than I am already, that I'm relieved she agrees with me, that she's taking me seriously. But I can't, because as glad as I am that she's listening, I am terrified.

So much for feeling like a normal girl again. That's all over, and I'm not sure I'll ever get it back. It feels so unfair. I know people don't get murdered—or almost murdered—only if they deserve it, but I don't understand what I've done that would even make someone *want* to. I stick mostly to my friends. I love gossip as much as the next person, but I don't spread it, only listen to it. I don't have any exes creepily pining for me, that I know of.

"Why me, Mom?" I ask, and then I start to cry.

I feel like a baby, crying while my mom hugs me and my brother sets a hand uncomfortably on my shoulder. I want to stop, but I can't. I'm already raw from crying earlier, and even more raw from admitting that I'm scared. The deepness of the emotions in my heart feel like mourning. I'm grieving for the person I was before, the person who's lost now, who was replaced by someone who knows that even here in my small corner of the world, things are not always safe. I miss not holding my breath every morning when Hunter drives us across the bridge into

Vermont for school. I miss my nonchalance about the water and the dams and anywhere I might be able to fall. My feeling that because I took swimming lessons from the time I was a toddler till I was in eighth grade, water can't hurt me. That arrogant ignorance, it was beautiful.

And now it's gone, gone, gone.

19

Mom calls the police as soon as I calm down, and she tells me I'm not going to school the next day. Hunter, either. Dad gets home tomorrow morning, and then we'll go talk to the St. Elm police in person, and the whole thing is starting to make me feel really panicked.

Sky and Liam come over after school. I'm not in the mood for either of them to be here, but I don't know why or how to tell them that, so I let them stay. Sky decides that we should hang out as a foursome and lets herself into Hunter's room to retrieve him. The familiar sounds of Fortnite blast from his open door and disappear when she shuts it behind her. I take Liam's hand and lead him into my room, because I have the feeling it'll be a little bit before Sky coaxes Hunter out of there.

"Hey, I found you something," Liam says.

He reaches into his coat pocket with an involuntary curl of his nose and pulls out a neatly folded tissue containing a diamond-shaped bug that's all black except its thorax, which is pale yellow surrounding a black splotch.

"Oh, an American carrion beetle! I don't actually have one in my collection yet."

A dead insect might seem like a super unromantic gift, but honestly he couldn't have given me anything better.

"I'm glad you like it." He kisses me. "But, um, I'm going to go wash my hands. Bugs are . . . well, you know."

He kisses me once more and slips out of my room.

While I pin the carrion bug carefully beside a green-striped grasshopper in my insect display, I think about how adorable it is that Liam's grossed out by bugs. I carefully orient the bug, turn, and am so startled I nearly trip over my own feet. Liam stands a couple of feet away, watching me with a weird smile.

"I still think the bug thing is pretty weird," he says. "But I also really love how much you love them."

Before I can respond, he's kissing me. His lips are a gentle pressure on mine. I slide a hand to the back of his head, kissing him more deeply. I twist my fingers in his hair, and let everything else about this crappy day fall aside.

"I'm so glad," he says, "that you finally decided to give me a chance."

"Me too." I wrap my arms tight around his neck, rest my chin on his shoulder. "And I'm glad you decided to like me even though you think my brother is a jerk."

I find myself looking deep into his bottomless ocean eyes and completely lose my breath. He kisses me again, and I don't care that my door is open and that my brother is probably coming in here any minute. I just want to absorb everything about this. I throw myself fully into this kiss, let myself feel everything about it a thousand times more intensely than I need to. Liam is so handsome and nice and thoughtful, I can hardly believe he belongs to me. I want everything else to be this easy, this *right*.

I want—

"Amelia!"

Hunter's disgusted voice really ruins the mood. Better him than Mom, though, I guess. Liam steps away from me with a sigh.

"You're dating my best friend" is the only retort I can come up with, even though Hunter is glaring at me with a strength he usually reserves for his computer screen if he thinks someone is cheating at Fortnite.

Sky loops her arms around his waist. "Chill," she tells him.

If I'd said that, it would not work. It would opposite of work. But Sky clearly has power over him now, because he softens his scowl and sits quietly on the corner of my bed. Sky sits beside Hunter, and I move to my beanbag chair near the window. Liam leans against the sill, towering over me.

"So, you wanna recap for us?" Sky asks.

"Not really." I feel like a wrung-out sponge, and knowing that I'll have to talk to police tomorrow, I don't want to get into everything now. The thought of it exhausts me to my marrow. "Did Hunter not already fill you in?"

She shakes her head.

"Well, there's not much to say, I guess. The deaths are starting to seem suspicious and Mom agreed that it looks like my accident was suspicious, too, and so did the police when she called them. So tomorrow I get to recount exactly what happened to me. Maybe I'll have to provide a list of my enemies." I try to lighten it at the end because I can tell I sound sour.

Liam frowns, but Sky gets it. "You're going to have to ask for a lot of paper," she teases.

I stick out my tongue. "I don't even think I have any true enemies, sadly. I need to join a sports team and form a rivalry."

"I don't recommend it," Hunter says dryly.

Liam rests his hand on my head and opens his mouth to respond but gets distracted by something outside. "That creepy guy is staring in here."

I wrinkle my nose. "Not surprised. But it's nice to know he's willing to stare at whoever stands in that window, even if it isn't me."

"Ew, really?" Hunter scowls. "How often does he do that?"

"I don't know. Pretty often. I close my blinds a lot."

"When did this start?" Hunter moves to the window, his scowl intensified, and lowers my blinds.

"Not that long ago."

"We should tell Mom."

"Hunter," I groan. "I already know he's a problem, but I feel like I talked to Mom about enough stuff already. I'm obviously going to mention him when I talk to the police."

Hunter tenses and looks to Sky for support. She shrugs. "Maybe there's been enough for today, you think?"

"You should be careful, though," Liam says. "He seems like the sort of person who would—"

"Yeah, I know."' It's more snappish than I meant it to be. I take a deep breath to calm down. "Sorry. I do watch out for him. I know something's not right there."

We lapse into a semi-comfortable silence, and I sort of wish Sky would lure Hunter back to his room so I can kiss Liam more. I'm about to subtly suggest it when Liam says, "Was that Fortnite I heard coming from your room earlier?"

Hunter looks suspicious. "Yeah, why?"

Liam shrugs. "Didn't know you played."

"*You* play?" Hunter's face is pure shock.

"Aw, look at that." I cannot contain my smugness. "Another hobby you have in common."

I can tell immediately that Hunter is going to seek revenge, and it's already too late. "That's true. And you want us to bond *so badly*, right? So *maybe* we should all go to my room and *together*, Liam and I can show you two how to play."

It's not that I don't like video games. I do. But I like them to have plot, and Fortnite . . . well, it doesn't.

"What have I done to deserve this suffering?" I ask, folding myself deeper into my beanbag chair.

"Oh come on." Liam reaches for my hand, tugs me up. "You did want us to become friends, you know."

"I changed my mind," I mutter.

Liam just laughs and drags me out of my room.

I don't want to admit it, but the four of us playing Fortnite was actually pretty fun. This is a secret I will keep to myself eternally, though.

I'm glad I didn't tell Liam not to come earlier when I didn't feel like seeing anyone, because it was nice having him here. My mom likes him; he was polite at dinnertime and helped with the dishes afterward, which is something I never do unless asked.

Sky's spending the night, but Liam left a little while ago, departing with a kiss so good it'll probably keep me feeling blissful all the way through tomorrow.

Once he's gone, I arrogantly point out to my brother that he didn't seem to mind having Liam here so much, and then I steal Sky into my room to analyze every moment of it.

"You know Roman was totally responsible for the two of you getting together, right?" she says while we paint each other's toes. I'm so happy she's here and I don't have to share her with Hunter right now. "He's been all about it ever since Liam started talking about you after your accident."

"I know, I know. I thought he was being totally nuts, but so far . . . it's going really well. And don't pretend *you* didn't push for this, too, even though Hunter hates it."

"Oh, Hunter's fine." She brushes my comment aside. "He'll come around. He's just stubborn. And I pushed for it because I could tell you liked him and I thought Liam deserved someone nice, too."

"Since when do you have opinions on Liam, anyway?" I carefully press a line of pink to the tip of her big toe. "You never talked to him any more than I did."

"No, but actually my dad mentions him sometimes. He owns land over near Liam's dad's hunting camp, and he's always thought Liam was nice and well-mannered and stuff. Not that he sees him often, but you know."

"And what does your dad think of Hunter?"

"Oh God." Sky rolls her eyes. "Well, he's never thought of him as well-mannered, that's for sure."

I laugh. "Good, because he's not."

"Isn't this adorable?" Sky waves her hand over my drying feet. "We're both dating hot soccer players."

"Excuse me. One of us is dating a hot soccer player and the other is dating a weirdo who maybe gave her some kind of love potion."

She laughs. "Come on, you know your brother is hot."

I mime vomiting. "You've got to stop."

"Fine, fine. But honestly I'm glad to see you happy. I mean, I know you're not *happy* with everything going on, but you've been kind of . . . Okay, correct me if I'm totally one thousand percent wrong or overstepping or whatever, but I've felt like maybe you've been pining for someone who seems to have been, like, oblivious to the pining? Maybe a friend of ours?" She is the embodiment of the grimacing emoji, and my stomach is one big wasp's nest.

"Which friend do you think I've been pining over?" I ask lightly. She can't possibly know. She can't.

"Ummm, maybe . . . Grace?"

She knows.

I can't believe this. First Tera brings it up at the craft fair, and now Sky, who's been totally focused on her own relationship, can tell?

"How did you . . . Did she say something? Or— God, was it super obvious?"

"No! No, I just kinda . . . I don't know. I picked up on it. Should I not have mentioned it?"

"No, it's fine. It's good, actually." I finish her toes and carefully cap the nail polish.

"Why didn't you tell me?" She bites her lip. "I mean, not that you're obligated to tell me anything, but . . . Ugh, I'm going about this all wrong, aren't I? I'm supposed to wait till you said something to me; I'm not supposed to just *ask*."

She rakes fingers through her hair, looking anguished at how she's unintentionally forced me to discuss this.

"No, it's totally fine. It's easier this way." I can't quite look her in the eye. "I don't know. I'm still figuring out . . . Like, what do I call myself, you know? And how am I only just realizing I feel this way, and why does my first real crush on a girl have to be one of my closest friends? I didn't know how to even say what I'm feeling, and it's been kind of on the back burner because of my accident and I'm with Liam, so does it even matter right now? I mean, maybe it matters. I don't know. I think I'm bisexual, but I'm still figuring it out and as you can tell, I have zero answers."

"Well, you don't have to have answers. You don't owe me or anyone an analysis of your feelings and what you think you should be labeled until and unless you want to. I just want . . . I know I kept my relationship with Hunter a secret, but I want you to still trust me."

"Oh, Sky, I do! Of course I do. It was more . . . *Grace* is the person who could best help me figure out how I feel, but she's also the person making me the most confused. So I . . . well, I talked to her about it and it was going fine, but then I told her I liked her and I got so embarrassed and I *fled*. And then I was even more embarrassed and we were so awkward and it finally has started to feel unawkward again, and I only kept it to myself so you wouldn't get sucked into the awkwardness, too. Sometimes I'm a total moron, Sky; you know this."

She scoots toward me, careful not to touch my sheets with her drying toes, and hugs me. "You are never a moron, Amelia. You're a person who had a crush and did something awkward, which means you are the same as literally everyone on the planet who's ever had a crush."

"That's true I guess." I squeeze her tight. "What would I do without you?"

"Oh, you'd be totally lost. But same, you know. I'd be, like, an empty husk without you." She lets me go. "You wanna talk about it at all?"

"I don't know. Maybe. I'm not sure what to say. I have a crush on Grace, I guess, which feels super weird to say out loud."

"Well, if you're going to have a crush, Grace is a pretty good choice."

"But it doesn't matter now, right? I mean, there's Liam."

"What would you do if she told you she was interested?"

Sky never lets me off easy. She is an asker of hard questions. Ones I don't want to think about, let alone answer. "I . . . Well, I wouldn't break up with Liam, not now, unless there were, like, other factors. Plus, dating someone who's been your friend for years is pretty fraught. I'd have to think very hard about if the risk was worth it. I would be so heartbroken to lose her altogether. Anyway, she's not interested, so there's that."

"True about the risk. And don't get me wrong, I think Liam's great for you, and I'm not trying to lead you in any direction. But transitioning with your brother from friends to people who make out was . . . easier than you'd think. Just saying."

"Message received. Now we better get to bed. I may not be going to school tomorrow, but you are."

"Psh, please. No way in hell I'm taking the bus. Besides, I want to be around when you get back from the police station. I already convinced my mom to call me in sick."

Sky isn't exactly student of the year. School's a thing she does because she has to, not because she enjoys it. School isn't something her parents care about, either. Her dad is always spouting about how *real men* don't need school because they have trades and don't require it. I get it, and I know it comes from a place of defensiveness, but taking that attitude doesn't seem any better to me than someone being elitist about having to go to *the exact right college* and become a CEO or something. Sky's parents' laxity about education has rubbed off on her. She doesn't skip school much, but when she wants to, she meets absolutely zero resistance.

After a few more minutes, I head to the bathroom at the end of the hall to brush my teeth. As I pass by the top of the stairs, I pause because I hear Mom's voice, and she sounds upset. I creep partway down the stairs as quietly as possible and listen.

"Did you ever think, when Jenna and I were kids—did it ever even remotely cross your mind to worry about the possibility of someone trying to kill one of us?"

She pauses to listen, and I realize with a jolt in my stomach that she's talking to Gram. My mom is getting advice from *her* mom, about me. I feel tremendously guilty, even knowing that none of this is my fault.

"I know it can happen anywhere but I— We live here so we don't have to worry about this stuff so much. I've worked so hard raising them to be good kids and they *are*, I just—"

She listens again. The silence is almost worse than listening to her speaking in a ragged-edged voice.

"You're right. No, they're both upstairs. I don't want her to know I'm upset, obviously. She's so worried, and I don't want to make it worse. But how do I even— I can't protect my kid, Mom. It's a pretty bad feeling. I don't want to stifle her, but right now I don't even want her to leave this house ever again. I can't— She's not safe out there and there's nothing I can do to protect her."

Her voice breaks, and I don't want to listen to it anymore. I edge back up the stairs as fast as I can and close myself into the bathroom, breathing deep to stave off tears. Mom's words hit on what upsets me most about all this: the shattered illusion of safety. Bad things have happened here. Bad things happen *everywhere*. But it's infrequent. That's a big part of the draw of our tiny little town. Roots run deep, and people are here for one another when it counts. But no one can save me from this. We can't have a dance or a spaghetti dinner or a firemen's breakfast to raise money for my cause. I can't be protected, because no one knows who to protect me *from*.

There's someone in this area who wants to see girls dead. Girls who have nothing in common beyond the fact that we're teenage girls. Someone who wanted me to let it go. But I can't, not now. I won't.

Because I *will not* be next.

20

The police station makes me sweaty. I feel like I'm in trouble even though I know it's super the opposite. Mom and Dad both came with me. I don't usually mind that Dad's not home a lot. It's our family's normal, and it makes the time when he's there more special. But with all this going on, I've been sort of wishing he didn't have to go back out on the road. It's not that there's anything he can do that Mom can't, but two parents feel safer than one, I guess.

Liam texted me a little while ago, a message of support and a photoshopped GIF of an ant lifting weights, which made me laugh. I also got a Where r uuuuu? text from Grace, who's in my first-period class. I asked Sky not to fill anyone in on what's up. I want to do it later, when I'm not feeling so tired and raw and frightened. I felt bad lying to Grace, but I told her I was sick and then put my phone away and haven't looked at it since.

They don't make us wait around; we go directly into the office of Detective Heather Cheney, the woman who agreed to speak with us. It's a bland, standard-looking office, but there are a lot of plants and pictures of someone who I assume is her daughter, and next to her computer monitor there's a cute stuffed chicken.

"So you had an accident a couple of months ago and were hospitalized with various injuries, is that right?" she asks.

I nod.

"And this happened behind the Comerford Dam? What were you doing over there? Walk me through the whole thing."

We're jumping right into it, I guess. I glance at Mom and Dad, both of whom smile encouragingly. Dad squeezes my hand.

And I recount everything I can remember. Driving down to the river because it's one of my favorite places to go for walks with Sky and because she wanted to tell me something important. Sitting on the guardrail, watching water thunder out the back of the dam. I get brave and tell her the three things I remember: the snap of my necklace chain, the feeling of a push on my shoulder, and the echo of laughter as I tumbled.

She digs into all of it. What was the thing Sky wanted to tell me? Had we gotten into any fights recently? Did I see anyone or anything strange? What makes me think it's connected to the other girls? Do I know them or their brothers? Does my *brother* know them or their brothers? How is my relationship with Hunter? With my other friends? Every detail about Mr. Omerton and the picture I "allegedly" saw in his house. The text I received that said to *let it go*. On and on, and then finally: "Is it okay if I talk to you alone for a minute?"

My throat goes dry. I don't want Mom and Dad to leave, but I'm a big girl. I can do this. "Yeah. It's fine."

She waits patiently while Mom and Dad exit the room and shut the door.

"Do you feel safe at home?" she asks. "Please remember to be honest, okay? I'm here to help."

I gaze levelly at her. "Are you asking if someone in my home might have tried to kill me?"

"No. I'm asking if you feel safe at home."

"Of course I do. Why would my parents have come with me to a police station if they were secretly hurting me?"

She smiles sadly. "Honey, it happens so much more often than you'd think."

I frown. "Well, that's terrible."

"Yes, it is. I think that's all I need for now. If I think of anything I forgot to ask, or if there are any developments you and your family should be let in on, I will be in contact. Okay?"

I thank her and leave, feeling kind of detached from reality. Mom and Dad take me to the grocery store to pick out whatever candy and ice cream my heart desires, and although it makes me feel like a little kid again, I'm also enjoying this time with them. I know they only want to distract me, but they're laughing, joking around with me, and it makes me feel less heavy than I felt talking to that detective in the police station. We go to the cash register with a huge package of gummy worms and two quarts of ice cream, and Mom says, "We also feed her vegetables, I swear," to the cashier, who looks unimpressed.

On the car ride home, I start thinking about things again. I think about everything I said to the detective, and I think about Mom crying on the phone with Gram.

"Thanks for taking me seriously about this stuff," I blurt out.

Mom glances in the rearview, and Dad turns in the passenger seat to face me. "Of course," he says. "We'll always take you seriously."

My throat feels tight. I know it's true, but hearing it really means something.

"I know you guys are worried about me now, but I . . . Are you going to, like, not want me to go places anymore?"

A brief silence, then Mom says, "We're not going to put you under house arrest, Amelia. We kind of can't, and it's not fair to you. Just promise you'll be careful, all right? *Beyond* careful. And let us know where you're going and when. If something seems like a bad idea, I'll tell you. Otherwise . . . we have to be business as usual. We can't keep you trapped in a glass tower, much as I wish we could."

"That is too bad," I say lightly. "Because a glass tower sounds fun and terrifying all at once."

Mom smiles at me in the rearview.

"One last time, though, I want to reiterate what Dad said: We will always be on your side. Don't be afraid to tell us something because you think we won't take it seriously. We will. We always, always will."

This is not the first time my parents have told me these

words. Since I was a small child first learning about bodies and consent in its most basic form, they've been telling me this. And I've always believed them. But I never thought there would come a time when I had to talk to them about something so serious as this. It was scaricr to do, in reality.

But now that it's over, I wish I'd said something so much sooner.

21

School over the next couple of weeks is surreal. Everyone knows, somehow, that I spoke with the police. I would blame the small town thing for this if I could, but with students from so many surrounding areas filtering into this one high school, it's just not that small. There are whispers everywhere: that Maria and Lydia were killed, that someone tried to do the same to me. I'm getting even more attention than before, and a different kind of attention. Before, I was a girl who survived what people thought was a dumb accident. Now, I'm a girl who survived a murder attempt. I'm cool, suddenly. I'm fascinating.

I hate it.

I have a new level of empathy for the insects I trap and observe in my little bug sanctuary. Caged and surrounded by a million magnifying glasses, stared at openly while people try to figure out how I work. Why someone would try to hurt me. Jealousy? Hate? Random coincidence? All questions I've been trying to answer for weeks, with zero success whatsoever.

I'm late for AP Biology because I get trapped in the

bathroom by a bunch of sophomore girls I don't even know who have a million invasive questions about my life. There's practically no one around as I sprint out of the English building, down the sidewalk, and across the street to the science building. It's funny, really, because I've grown to hate having other people around me, but solitude is terrifying, too. I'm in a no-win situation that I've done absolutely nothing to deserve.

I'm almost to my classroom when I hear it, coming from a clover-shaped cluster of lockers at the center of the building's main floor.

Someone's crying.

I should ignore it and go to class, but I've gotten soft. So instead, I investigate. I almost change my mind when I see who it is: Steve Lugen. Sitting alone with his back against the lockers and his knees pulled to his chest. Don't get me wrong; I have absolutely no problem with Steve. I just don't know what to say to him, and I feel like I probably *should* have said something a long while ago.

But it's too late to escape. He sees me, stiffens, and scrambles to his feet.

"I'm sorry," I say. "I— Are you okay?"

"I'm great, obviously," he snaps. "Soon to be even better when you tell the whole school you saw me crying."

"Why would I tell anyone that?"

"I don't know. Maybe you wouldn't. But everyone seems to think my whole life is their business these days, so."

"Tell me about it."

His defensiveness melts away. "You too, huh?"

"Well, I am the Girl Who Lived."

I hope he gets my Harry Potter reference, otherwise that probably comes off flippant and jerkish. His half-hearted smile tells me that he understands.

"Are you a good person?" he asks.

I'm taken completely off guard. "I—I guess? I don't know. I try to be."

"Maria was a really good person, you know. I'm not. I mean, I'm not evil or anything like that, but I'm just . . . I'm not that nice to people. Maria was nice to everyone. It seems like— Why *her*? It doesn't seem fair, and I hope that you—"

"I would rather you just don't finish that sentence," I interrupt. "I came over here because I heard crying and I wanted to make sure whoever it was was okay. This whole living and dying thing, it's not a competition of merit. Otherwise, Maria would be here today and our attacker would not. I'm sorry that she was killed, so *unbelievably* sorry, but I'm not going to tell you I wish I'd died in her place. I'm not going to try to prove to you that I deserve to be here right now, because there's nothing to prove."

I start to turn away, but I've made him angry now, and he blocks me off. "You think you're so great, don't you? Just because you're smart and your brother's good at soccer and your family's some kind of Maple Hill royalty, you think you deserve more than everybody else."

"I'm sorry, are you *kidding* me?"

It's not the first time I've heard this Maple Hill royalty crap or some variation thereof. Not always directed at me. It happens a lot in all the towns around here, where people assume that other families are more highly regarded than theirs are, and it's almost never true. There are a few families who have been rooted in Maple Hill since the beginning of time, and I'm not related to any of them. But if your family's at all involved in town politics—which mine is—people love to assume it means they think they're better than everyone else. It's stupid. If everyone took that attitude and no one got involved, nothing would be taken care of. Our town wouldn't be able to function. And most important of all: Steve lives in Hen Falls. His family has been there for generations. The church was so packed for Maria's funeral, they had to ask tons of people to stay outside because otherwise it would break fire code.

So, basically, everything he just said is completely hypocritical.

"Don't pretend you came over here to do anything but parade yourself in front of my face."

"Are you serious? What is *wrong* with you?" Tears burn hot behind my eyes, and it takes everything I've got to hold them in, because I don't want him to see me visibly upset. I know why he's taking this out on me, but I'm not strong enough to let myself be his punching bag. I'm still too scared, still too close to this whole situation.

"Get out of here," says a voice behind me.

It's Tera, glaring daggers at Steve. Tera's a scary girl,

honestly. She knows how to wear a scowl, and she's not afraid to throw a punch.

For a second, it seems like Steve is considering yelling at her, too, but instead he shoves past me and storms off.

"You okay?" Tera asks, reaching for my arm.

That's when I realize I'm shaking pretty badly. "I'm fine. He's just upset, and I shouldn't have even tried to talk to him at all. I heard crying and I didn't know it was him . . ." I adjust my glasses, rake my fingers through my hair. "Where did you come from?"

"Mrs. Marecaux sent me," she says. "Since she knows we're friends and she thought it was unusual that you weren't in class."

"And what, exactly, was her plan for if you found me murdered in a bathroom?"

Tera narrows her eyes, hands on her hips. "Not super funny, you know."

"I know, I'm sorry. It's just laugh or cry, honestly."

She wraps her arms around me, and I lean my head against her shoulder.

"Don't let Steve get to you too much, okay? Roman told me he's always been a little jerk. I'm sure Liam would say the same—I know they've talked about it. Just because there's reason for him to be upset now doesn't give him the right to talk to you like that. And he's only thinking of all this from his own perspective. He's not thinking about what it must feel like to be you and to still be scared."

"I'm trying to give him the benefit of the doubt, though,"

I tell her. "Because I do get it. I totally get it. If Hunter died and someone else lived through the same thing . . . I would know it wasn't their fault, but I'm pretty sure I'd hate them anyway."

"You're a really nice, good person, Amelia, and I respect the hell out of that." Tera squeezes me. "But you know what? Screw Steve. I only heard the tail end of that, but he's garbage to me now."

That makes me laugh. Tera's a good friend. Loyal to the core.

I *am* trying to give Steve the benefit of the doubt, but also, he's not totally wrong about me. It's horrid to hold yourself up against someone else, but if I hold myself up against Maria or Lydia, I easily come in third. I'm not a bad person and I'm happy with who I am, but I can be real petty at times. I kind of like it when someone I dislike doesn't get their way. I like it when Mom and Aunt Jenna talk about other adults in town, because I enjoy hearing the gossip.

I'm flawed. We all are, obviously. But if I were going to pick one of the three of us to live . . . I don't know. This is a bad path for my mind to take, and I wish Steve hadn't said anything.

"I have good taste in friends," I tell her. "That might be my best trait."

Tera laughs and hugs me again. "Can't argue with you there. Now let's get to class before Mrs. Marecaux thinks we were *both* murdered in a bathroom."

"Steve's a pile of crap," says Liam, not mincing words.

Hunter's doing something for his senior capstone project, so

I'm stuck at school for a half hour or so before we can go home. Sky went with Hunter because that's what she does now, but Liam's hanging out with me in the athletic building—a place where we both spend way too much time and therefore feel most comfortable. We're sitting at the top of the bleachers surrounding the empty basketball court, and I've told him every detail of my encounter with Steve.

"Sorry," he adds, "I know he's having a hard time and I should be understanding, but I don't like him."

"He's, like, a *lot* younger than you, though; when have you even interacted with him?"

"His parents are the ones who started the rumor that my dad murdered my mom and buried her in the woods somewhere." Liam's tone is beyond bitter. "And Steve's the one who made sure the entirety of Hen Falls Elementary heard that story."

"All right. That concludes it. He's a pile of crap."

Liam laughs. "Hey, I have something for you. I almost forgot."

"Is it another carrion beetle? Where'd you get that, by the way?"

Liam pauses mid-rummage through his backpack. "Get what? The beetle?"

"Yeah. They eat corpses, that's where they're usually found."

"Oh. It was on my lawn near the road. Probably came off a dead squirrel or some other roadkill."

"Makes sense."

"Makes me extra glad I washed my hands after I touched it." He grins, and then holds something out to me in a clenched fist. "Listen, I know how much you liked that necklace. I remember you wearing it, and I felt bad that you missed it so much. So I went online, and I found you one that I think is pretty similar."

He opens his fist, and there sits . . . my necklace.

I pluck it gingerly from his palm. The chain is different— more delicate, and it's not silver—but the rectangle of wood, it's not just "pretty similar." It's literally my necklace. All the different shades of wood scrap are in the same spot. It has the same dings around the edges. The same imprint on the bottom where they tightened the clamp too much while the glue dried.

"Liam, where did you get this? This is *my* pendant. The very same one. How did someone have this for sale?"

"It's not the exact same one," he protests. "There's no way. Anyway I got it off an Etsy shop, and the lady lives in Arkansas."

I don't want to argue with him, but something isn't adding up here at all. I've worn this pendant every day for years. I know it like I know my own skin.

"Thank you," I whisper.

He smiles at me, bright and perfect, and clasps the necklace around my throat. It feels *right*, like a piece of me that's been missing, but also *wrong* because the chain's different and it sits differently on my chest, and because nothing can just be uncomplicated, ever since my accident.

I squeeze my fist around the rectangle of wood and breathe a long, slow sigh.

I don't know how Liam got my necklace back, and I don't think I *want* to know. But regardless of anything else, I'm so glad I have it.

"Where'd you get that?" Hunter demands the second I get into the car.

"Liam bought it off Etsy," I answer. It feels like a lie rolling off my tongue, even though it isn't. Liam showed me the store on his phone, and the lady in Arkansas really does sell wood jewelry just like this. Except, well, this one is *mine*.

"Maybe the chain," Hunter says, "but I made that thing, remember? I know what it looks like."

I clutch the necklace in my fist and shrug. He and Sky exchange a glance in the front seat, and I can tell I'm not going to like whatever I'm about to hear.

"Amelia, Hunter and I have been talking," Sky begins. "And he told me something about Liam that's a little . . . worrying."

"Oh, you mean there's an *actual* reason you hate him so much, not the weak excuse you made up when you lied to me?" I snap. I'm being rude, but I feel defensive and teamed up on.

"Yes," says Hunter coolly. "And I didn't want to say anything because I was trying not to be a jerk and I know we all make mistakes, but I mean, where did he get that necklace? How did he have it? Why is he— Just listen. He and I were at the same soccer camp one summer, in middle school. And please do not tell him I told you this, okay?"

"Okay," I say sullenly. I don't like that Hunter's trying to drag my boyfriend through the mud, but also I'm not going to *not* listen to this.

"It was late at night and I'd snuck out of my cabin because I had to use the bathroom. I didn't want to go all the way to the actual bathroom because, you know, why walk that far when you can just pee into nature." He's trying to lighten the mood, but I'm not laughing. "And I went into the woods a little bit, and I saw Liam with . . . There was a whole bunch of dead squirrels at the base of a tree all laid out in this neat row with their tails curled perfectly over their backs, and he was . . . Well, to be honest I don't know exactly what he was doing with them before I got there, because he'd clearly heard me coming. He told me he'd found them like that and was just looking."

"And you think what? *He* killed a pile of squirrels?"

"I don't know! I mean, maybe he did just find them there, but something about it always, *always* felt off to me, Amelia. What was he doing out there in the middle of the night? How did he happen to find this incredibly weird thing, and when I asked if he wanted to walk back to the cabins together, why did he say no? Why did he want to stay there looking at those perfectly arranged squirrels? It was disturbing, and I've never forgotten it."

"Oh come *on*, Hunter." His story combined with this necklace weirdness isn't sitting well with me at all, but I've reached the limit of what I can take, and I feel myself snapping. "This was so many years ago and you already didn't like him; you don't think you might be choosing not to give him the benefit of the doubt simply because you're not a fan?"

"He's just saying you should be careful with Liam," says Sky.

"*You* are the one who pushed me toward him in the first place," I snarl. "Because according to your dad, he's the absolute best. Did you tell Hunter *that* during the one billion hours you've spent together, talking about me, apparently, and what's best for me? But not including me, because why would you bother?"

"I didn't know this story, Amelia, and you're not being very fair right now."

"No? So you *haven't* been prioritizing plans with Hunter over plans with me for months now? My mistake."

"I'm not going to dignify that with a response."

"Because you know I'm right!"

"Fine, be mad at us." She whips around in her seat and glares at me. "Whatever, Amelia. Just please at least think about what Hunter is telling you and whether you should be giving it just a *touch* more thought than you are right now."

I don't dignify *that* with a response. I slump in my seat and glare out the window until we get home. Then I slam upstairs and lock my bedroom and close my blinds and fall face-first onto my bed, where I scream into my pillow.

It doesn't fix anything.

22

Are u allowed out?

It's Saturday, and I wake to this text from Grace.

Yes, why?

We won't talk about how long it takes for me to think up that response. I'm going to go ahead and blame the fact that I just woke up, even though it's not exactly the crack of dawn.

Idk, I thought you might like to do something . . . normal & indoorsy. Shopping?

YES.

Should I see if Tera wants to come? & Sky?

Sky & Hunter have plans today 😩 but yes check with Tera! I can drive us obv.

At least, I better be able to. I'm technically allowed to drive now, but I haven't done it yet. I hop out of bed, invigorated by the idea of getting out of this town, this whole *area* for a little while. Because when Grace asks if I want to go shopping, she doesn't mean at the postapocalyptic wasteland that passes for a mall in St. Elm, with its one nice department store and its eerie, mostly empty corridors. No, she means driving a couple of hours to Burlington, where they have actual stores.

I haven't spoken to Sky since our fight, and I haven't spoken to Hunter either, except when I have to. Our car rides home from school have been absolutely glacial, but I am not going to be the one who apologizes first. The fact that Liam managed to find my exact necklace is definitely weird, but he's been more supportive and helpful than anyone else throughout all of this. I have to trust that he has his reasons for not telling me how he got that necklace back. My guess is he went searching behind the dam, which is phenomenally stupid but also extremely kind.

None of my friends—except Liam, and I didn't tell him the whole truth about *why*—even knows I'm fighting with Sky, though. I don't want anyone to feel like they have to start taking sides.

I explode downstairs in my T-shirt and pajama shorts, skipping the last four steps and landing at the bottom just at the right moment to scare the crap out of my mom, who happens to be walking by.

"You're going to give me a heart attack one of these days," she says, pressing a hand to her chest.

"Sorry. Can I take the car? Grace and maybe Tera want to go to Burlington."

I can practically see the war in Mom's eyes. She doesn't want me to go—there or anywhere—but she also doesn't want to coop me up in the house and push me into a boredom-induced bad decision. I hold my breath and try to look as adorable as possible so she'll give in.

"Drive *extremely carefully*," she says, and I shriek and hug her. "I mean it, Amelia. Do not drive like your father and me. Drive like your grandmother. And if you feel even *the tiniest bit dizzy*, pull over and switch with one of your friends."

Gram is a very cautious driver and may never have exceeded the speed limit in her life. Mom, on the other hand, drives like she's in a high-speed car chase. And Dad is even worse.

"What are you talking about!" he protests from the living room. "I am a professional driver!"

This is what he says anytime Mom comments on his bat-out-of-hell habits.

"I will drive like Gram," I promise. "Or . . . close enough, at least."

That earns me a chuckle from both Mom and Dad.

"Fair enough," says Mom. "But hey—if we're not home when you get back, we have a meeting tonight with the select-men. Text me before you leave Burlington, and text me when you get home, okay?"

"Okay. I thought they met on Tuesdays, though?"

"They do. This is a special meeting. People want to set up a, um, neighborhood watch type thing."

My stomach plummets. "Like, they want to watch me, basically?"

"Not from our backyard or anything." Mom folds her arms. "People are just really worked up about this. They're worried for you, of course, but also for the other teen girls in town. Think of this as a nice thing, Amelia, not a nuisance. No one will invade your privacy, I promise."

I don't like the idea of people neighborhood-watching me, but whatever. I'm not going to complain about it, because I can already tell from the fact that Mom didn't bring it up till now, and from the way she's talking about it, that she thinks this is a great idea.

"It's fine, Mom," I tell her, and I'm sure she can sense I don't really feel that way, but she doesn't say anything else. And neither do I, because I have some *being normal* to do.

The drive to Burlington never feels long when you aren't alone. I pick up both Tera and Grace from Grace's dorm—Tera lives near the school and hates people coming to her apartment and potentially interacting with her not-so-great mom. They spend most of the ride squabbling over what kind of music we should listen to, and finally I overrule them, turning on the '90s station that I've been Stockholm syndromed into liking by my mom, who listens to it all the time. (She also loves to tell me what songs she used to have *on cassette tape* or which ones she recorded onto a blank tape using her clock radio. She seems to really enjoy painting herself as some kind of ancient relic, no matter how little interest Hunter and I show in this cassette tape nonsense.)

The roads are clear, but a dusting of snow covers the rest of the ground, making for picturesque scenery on our trip. I feel relaxed and entirely unafraid for the first time in a long while.

Our first stop is Plato's Closet, and it's not too busy today, thankfully. After we load up our baskets, all three of us are able to get adjacent changing rooms. Tera, as usual, announces her feelings about everything she tries on loud enough for the whole store to hear.

"Nothing has ever looked worse on anybody than this shirt!" she shouts.

"Then don't buy it!" Grace shouts back.

"I'm putting it in the maybe pile."

Grace and I both laugh. I'm sure everyone else in the store is annoyed by us, but I don't care. My phone buzzes with a text message alert.

There's a beetle in my changing room come tell me if it's going to murder me.

The text is from Grace. I laugh and emerge in the outfit I was trying on. She's already got her door open and lets me in with a smile. "I like this," I tell her, gesturing to the high-waisted jeans and crop top combo she's trying on.

"Me too." She glances at herself in the mirror. "But it's kind of a waste of money, isn't it? I can't wear it to school."

Sometimes I wonder why she cares about wasting small amounts of money when her parents have so much of it, but then I think maybe if all rich people were this responsible, we'd have fewer problems.

"Where's the beetle?"

She points to the floor near her feet. I crouch beside it. Black, shiny, hard-shelled, oval. It's an easy one.

"That's a black carpet beetle," I tell her. "I find them cute, but they're kind of a menace."

"Should I squish it?"

I do it for her, grinding it into the carpet with the toe of my sneaker. I feel a tiny bit bad killing the thing, but they're destructive, and if a bug's destructive, I don't free it.

"You're my hero," she says, grinning. "And you should buy that shirt."

Her gaze lingers, and I feel it in my stomach. I am definitely buying this shirt.

"Hey, while you're here," she says in a low voice, "I want to update you on the maybe-stalker."

"Yeah? I wish your update was that there isn't one."

"Me too." She frowns. "I've been trying to be really careful and not, like, walk alone too much, but last night I went to Tera's and I didn't want to make her walk me back, because then *she* would be walking alone in the dark, which didn't feel any better. When I was like halfway home, I started to get the creepy feeling, so I walked faster. And then I definitely, one hundred percent, heard footsteps behind me. But when I turned around, they'd stopped. Like, straight out of a horror movie. I took out my keys and my pepper spray and I started just . . . sprinting. I'm sure people saw me and thought I looked like an idiot, but whatever. I could still hear footsteps after that, but I made it back to my dorm before whoever it was caught up to me."

"So someone really is . . ." I swallow hard. "Why don't you just take some space from me for a while, honestly? I don't know who's after me and why they would also be after you, but you'd be so much safer."

"They'd know," she says, and her voice is fierce. "And I don't want to stop being friends with you. I'm not going to be forced into it."

"Can I at least give your phone number to that detective I talked to? I've been texting her updates, like, constantly, even when nothing's happening to me. I'm sure she'd be interested."

"Yeah, okay. That's a good idea."

A knock on the changing room door startles us both. "Losers!" Tera says from the other side. "If you're going to share a dressing room, you gotta tell me."

Grace opens the door for her, laughing. "There was a bug situation. I thought you would probably make a scene."

"I absolutely would have." Tera's lips curve into a smile. "But the bug's gone, right? Let's all change in one room and harshly judge each other's outfits."

I hesitate, because the idea of changing in front of Grace now has taken on a new weirdness, but I'm trying to be normal today. Like none of this crap ever happened. So, I'm going to be normal.

"All right," I say, "I'll go get the rest of my clothes."

When we return from our trip, I drop off Tera first. She rockets out of the car with her purchases, and I leave as soon as she's in her apartment building just in case her mom comes out. I've met her mom plenty of times and she's not a *bad* person; she's just . . . troubled. But Tera doesn't like it when she interacts with friends. I don't blame her.

The atmosphere in the car becomes noticeably tenser and I don't know why. It feels like Grace wants to say something; she keeps fidgeting with her bracelet and her earrings, and biting her lip, which isn't something she usually does.

"Did you get everything you wanted?" I ask as we pull back onto Main Street.

"And then some." Her mouth twists into a half smile.

I turn into the driveway where the dorms are located and park in front of hers.

"Do you want help bringing in your bags?" I ask.

"No." She bites her lip again. "I want to tell you something, though."

She reaches into the back seat and gathers up her bags, holding them on her lap. I just wait.

"You know that day when you talked to me?" she says. I don't need to ask which day. I just nod. "Well, you kind of, like, ran away before I could say anything and I . . . I wish you had waited. That's . . . all I wanted to say."

My heart is in my throat, and I don't think I can speak, but it doesn't matter, because she's gone in a flash.

I watch her until she's inside the dorm, adjust my glasses three times, and only then am able to summon the will to drive away.

23

I'm restless. When I got home from shopping, Mom told me all about their meeting with the other townspeople and how everyone is basically just going to be on the lookout for me and the other teen girls in town, and also on the lookout for any "suspicious" people. Mom told people individually after the meeting to keep a particular eye on Mr. Omerton, without telling them any of the details I told the police. This all seems like a recipe for disaster, but at the same time, it probably won't be the worst thing to know there are eyes on me.

But then there's also Grace.

Sky asked me what I would do if it turned out Grace liked me, but I didn't consider it a possible scenario, so I didn't put any actual deep thought into my answer. I like Liam so much and I'm obviously not going to break up with him, but the idea that I could be with Grace if I wanted to is quite frankly thrilling. It would mean telling my family members—and everyone, I guess, when they saw us together—that I'm not straight, and that makes me a little nervous. Most people wouldn't care, but there will always be jerks out there, and there will always be those who just fundamentally don't understand bisexuality. Who can't get behind the very concept of being attracted to both boys and girls, and want you to pick one or the other. I would be okay, ultimately, though. The thought of telling people isn't frightening enough to stop me from dating her. I find myself scrolling through her Instagram again, almost as though my hands are moving independently of my brain.

She's just so . . . effortlessly stunning.

I set my phone down with a flash of guilt. Thinking about Grace like this when I'm dating Liam feels . . . I'm so torn. I need to see him.

U home? I text him.

It's midnight so . . . yes, obv.

I cringe. I didn't even look at the clock before texting him. Did I wake u?

No. Something wrong?

I just want to see u.

Come to my house? I can meet u by the bridge.

Sneaking out. Not something I've done before. Not something I *should* do. But . . .

Ok. Leaving now!

I tiptoe into the hallway, closing my door softly behind me. There's no glow beneath Hunter's door, and the downstairs is pitch-black, too. I grab my coat and some gloves and slip outside. On the porch, I hesitate for a second, because Mom and Dad would absolutely lose it if they found out I did this. They're taking my safety so extra seriously now—the whole town is. Dad's having security cameras installed and everything. But I *need* to see Liam.

Clutching my phone and using its flashlight app, I start down the road. I make it pretty far before I start to get completely creeped out. All the way to the library. But then I start to panic. I can't cross the bridge *on foot* at night. There's no way. If someone's after me and wants to throw me in that water, Liam won't be able to save me. No one knows I left the house; they won't even know where to *look* for me.

I whip around and run home as fast as I can. When I get back to my bedroom, I immediately start crying. I can't believe I was so stupid as to go outside at night in the pitch damn dark and freezing cold. Knowing there's a serial killer out there who's watching, waiting.

Just because the other incidents happened in rivers doesn't mean the killer won't become desperate enough to off me someplace else. They've been stalking Grace in the middle of St. Elm, after all.

My phone buzzes. A text from Liam. Where are you?? You ok??

Back home. So sorry, I just couldn't. Leaving my house at night was so dumb Liam. What was I thinking.

Ur not dumb. I'm coming there. Is that ok?

I think about it. If Mom finds him in my room, a serial killer is no longer my biggest worry. But at the same time . . . I really want to see him. I'm desperate to see him. I'm heavy with guilt over Grace's confession and how tempted it makes me. I wonder if I should tell Liam, and I decide not to. It would make me feel better not to feel like I'm carrying an ugly secret, but it would cause him unnecessary insecurity and hurt. That's not fair. It's selfish. So I won't do it.

Yes. Pls.

I wait, less patiently than I'd like to admit. When Liam texts that he's outside, I sneak down and let him in. It's risky, but I guess it's also good that there isn't a way for him (or anyone) to just climb into my room.

We make it through the living room, up the stairs, down the hallway, and then just as I'm about to close my door, Hunter opens his. He's sleep bleary and zombielike, obviously headed for the bathroom and not expecting to see anyone. At the sight of Liam beside me, his eyes widen, and he whispers a scandalized *"Amelia!"*

"We're not doing anything we shouldn't," I say quickly. "Please don't tell Mom and Dad. I just wanted to see him."

Hunter lingers, indecisive. "Fine, but if I find out that you—"

"We won't," I interrupt. I don't need to hear how that sentence ends.

He glares at Liam for a moment, then shuffles away toward the bathroom.

"That would've gone way worse if he hadn't been half asleep," I say after my door clicks shut. "Don't add stealth to my list of skills, I guess."

Liam laughs. "I don't know. You did pretty well. You just can't predict that brother of yours."

"True enough." Now that we're alone—*alone*, alone—I think about what that really means. Liam's arms are already around me, and a thrill sparks through me. No one will know what happens in here except us. What we say, what we do. It's a private, quiet moment, and what we make it is up to us.

"You know I meant it, what I told Hunter," I whisper. "I'm not quite ready to—"

"I understand." He lets go of me, unzips the jacket he's wearing, drapes it neatly over the back of my desk chair, and stacks his gloves and baseball cap on top of it. He almost looks annoyed for a moment, but then he fixes me with a brilliant smile and says, "I just wanted to see you, too."

"Good." I wrap my arms around him, nestle my face against his neck. I hate that I let Hunter talk me out of even *speaking* to Liam for so long, and I'm glad I let myself go for it in the end. I press my lips to his throat and revel in the fluttering inside of me when his arms tighten and he lets out a contented sigh. He captures my mouth with his, kissing me the way he does that makes me feel so *wanted*. I can barely breathe, but I don't care, because all I want is this: Liam, warming me from the inside out. Making me forget about the fear and the water and the murders. Mostly forget. Briefly forget.

"Liam," I whisper, pressing my forehead against his while I catch my breath. "I just feel . . . I'm scared. All the time."

He kisses me again, gently. "I won't let anything happen to you."

He can't promise that, as much as he might want to. He doesn't know what kind of person we're dealing with. No one does. The murderer might chalk me up to a mistake and leave me alone forever, or they might be watching me when I don't even know it. Goose bumps pucker my skin and I take a deep, steadying breath. Maybe he can't promise, but I know he means it. He wants to keep me safe, but he isn't trying to smother me. And that's something I can appreciate. I already have parents, and I don't need Sky and Hunter becoming a second set. I need people to trust me, to let me live my life. If I sit caged in my room, never leaving for fear of someone coming after me, then I may as well have died to begin with. Because that's not living.

I don't know exactly how to find the balance between caution and joy, but I intend to figure it out. And I have to be allowed to do it.

Liam brushes my hair lightly away from my neck with his fingertips, and then his lips graze my throat. His fingers tangle more tightly in my hair and he says, "Do you trust me?"

I pull his mouth to mine because right now kissing him is the thing I need. His kiss is the oxygen I breathe, and his arms around me are what hold me together.

"I trust you," I whisper.

His smile when he kisses me again—it's perfect.

24

In the morning, I get another text from the burner phone number. It's a picture of Liam outside my house in the dark, with the caption:

Pretty boyfriend. Does he know you'll be dead soon?

I show Mom immediately and then screenshot and send it to Detective Cheney. Mom wants me to stay home from school, but I talk her out of it. Her worry is a double-edged sword—I had to tell her Liam came here last night, but she's not even mad about that. She's just worried about his safety and wants to call his dad.

"I don't think his dad will care," says Hunter, surprising me. "I've never heard him say anything that wasn't a criticism to Liam, and anytime he actually comes to anything at school, he's scowling."

This information jolts me. What Hunter said isn't *news*, exactly, but it's a level of detail that I hadn't attained about Liam's dad. And Hunter doesn't even *like* Liam. It makes me think about how centered I've been on myself, how I've actually asked Liam next to nothing about his home life, telling myself that if he wanted to share, he would, and I feel like a jerk for that. Our relationship feels so real and important and beautiful, but have I even bothered to get to know him on a deep level? I've been so wrapped up in what's going on with *me* that my interactions with everyone around me have been . . . not superficial, exactly, but I certainly haven't been asking about *their* lives nearly as much as I should.

"I'll ask him," I tell Mom. "I'm sure he'll give me his dad's number for you."

At school, I abandon Hunter in the athletic building as soon as I see Liam. There's still plenty of time before morning assembly, so I take him to the stairwell that leads down to the pool, the famed ideal location for private conversations (or make-out sessions).

I show him the text I got, and he is, of course, outraged.

"The police really weren't able to trace the number?" he asks.

I shake my head. "And the messages are too short and generic to try to glean, like, a style from them. My mom was worried this might put you in danger, and she wants to call your dad. Is that possible?"

His expression darkens. "I'm not in danger. Only girls have died."

"Sure, so far, but we don't know what the killer might do with boyfriends of survivors. I know that sounds flippant, but seriously, we don't."

"Your mom does not need to talk to my dad, Amelia."

I'm annoyed by him brushing this off so much. "Maybe not, but what's the harm if she does?" When he doesn't say anything right away, I bluster on. "Is there a reason you don't want your dad hearing from my mom? I feel like . . . maybe I've been too self-absorbed lately and I just . . . I don't feel like I know enough deep stuff about your life. Do you feel that way?"

"Are you telling me you don't think we have deep conversations?" His voice rises. "Or maybe what you're actually telling me is that you don't listen when I speak."

I open and close my mouth. My face feels hot. We haven't fought yet and it had to happen eventually. But I don't like the look in his eyes, the flashing anger. It makes me think about what Hunter said about the squirrels, lined up all neatly.

"No, I'm not saying that. I *do* listen, and *obviously* we talk about stuff, but you've told me basically nothing about your family, Liam. All you've said is what people *think* of your parents, not what the truth is. So why don't you tell me why my mom can't call your dad?"

"Because he is a complete monster. Is that what you want to hear?" He's not shouting, but it *feels* like shouting. I find myself compelled to inch away from him, and something about that seems really wrong. "Why do you think I've never had you over to my house? Why do you think you didn't see him at a single one of my soccer games this season? He couldn't even muster interest in the *championship* for Christ's sake. He cares about nothing and no one except himself, and if your mom calls to tell him a serial killer might target me, he'll probably tell her *who cares.*"

My throat tightens. "I had no idea."

"Of course you didn't," he says gruffly. "I didn't *want* you to have any idea, but you pressed it, so there you go."

"Liam—"

I start to reach for him as he storms away, but something stops me. He doesn't want to be followed, that much is *very* clear.

Just the start to another super great day of school, I guess.

I don't hear from Liam until nine o'clock at night. To be fair, the silent treatment went both ways. But still.

I'm sorry about this morning. I shouldn't have gotten so mad at you.

It's fine, I understand.

It's not fine, though. I can't stop thinking about our fight. It wasn't the worst fight I've ever had. It wasn't the loudest or the cruelest. Steve was unkinder to me last week, even. But the *feeling* I got when he was angry with me. That impulse to step back, the voice in my head that screamed I wasn't safe. What was that? It felt important. It felt like a message I needed to heed.

Wouldn't it be funny, whispers a nasty voice in my head, *if you've been dating the serial killer all along?*

That voice turns wheels that I suddenly wish were left unturned. Liam's not the serial killer. No *way* is he the serial killer. To date me after trying to kill me would be so beyond sick. But also . . . he has hated Hunter for years. Then there's the death of Alec's sister shortly after he tried to lure me away from Liam at the Halloween party. And Steve spread rumors all over Hen Falls Elementary about Liam's dad. Three boys he hates, three sisters who were killed or almost killed. He also knows I missed seeing his championship game-winning goal because of Grace. Who started being followed shortly after that night. A dark family history and an absence of parental affection. A necklace that reappeared out of nowhere. Neatly arranged rows of dead squirrels in middle school. A dead beetle he gifted to me that's usually found on corpses.

No. I'm not going down this path. I'm completely overreacting to an incredibly minor fight.

Aren't I?

My phone screen lights up—he's calling me now. I reject it on impulse, not ready to talk to him while I'm working through whatever I'm feeling right now. I'm trying to think of a good excuse I can text him as to why I didn't answer when an excuse presents itself right outside my window: police sirens and flashing blue lights.

I move to my window and lift the blinds. There are four police cars parked in front of my neighbor's house. I snap a picture and text it to Liam with the message, Something's happening, call u in a bit.

WHOA!!! is what comes back.

I squeeze my phone between both palms, barely noticing when Hunter busts into my room without knocking.

"What's going on?" he asks.

"It looks like they're arresting Mr. Omerton."

I move so he can stand beside me.

"Do you think he's the one who . . . ?"

I can barely breathe. "I don't know. Maybe? What else would they be arresting him for?"

We both watch as Mr. Omerton emerges from his house, hands in the air. It's over so quickly. There is no standoff, no shouting, nothing. I don't know what I expected. This could be it. All my worries could end with this arrest. I wish that made me feel better. I wish it made me feel *anything*.

I stand in the window long after the flashing lights and the sirens have faded away, waiting for that feeling to come.

But it never does.

25

Turns out, I'm not the only one Mr. Omerton's been staring at lately. One of the neighborhood watch people noticed him at the library, spying on girls in the YA section. It's a pretty small thing, really, but between that and what I'd already shared, they decided it was worth looking into him and found some disturbing stuff. After the arrest, I had to go talk to Detective Chency again, but she wouldn't tell me any details about what they'd found as it was "not my business." I, personally, think it extremely *is* my business, but Mom pointed out that Detective Cheney has to follow the law and that this is all part of an ongoing investigation. The only thing I know is that they found pictures of Lydia and Maria and me on his computer—among others—plus several high school photos (including the one of me) and that he's charged with the two murders, and with my attempted murder.

My parents are absolutely elated. Everyone is.

Everyone except me.

Maybe he did it. I guess I *hope* he did it. But I don't *feel* like he did it.

"What do you want to do this weekend?" Liam asks me. We're over our fight—other than my lingering unsettled feeling—and we're walking together to class from morning assembly, fingers entwined.

"I don't know. I guess I can kind of do anything now, huh?"

He grins, his smile as disarmingly beautiful as ever. "Must feel pretty good."

I return the smile and lean into his arm as we walk. "It does feel good."

Saying it doesn't make it feel true, but my hope is that eventually it'll start to. Mr. Omerton's arrest just seems . . . too easy. I'm relieved he's behind bars, but it's hard to let go of the tension, the fear. Mom suggested therapy to me again last night, and this time I'm thinking I should take her up on it.

"Maybe we should go to the dam," Liam says. "If you're ready. I just . . . know you love it there, and it bums me out that you haven't been in months."

"I don't know." My fingers tighten around his. "Let me think about it?"

"Of course." He kisses me goodbye outside my English classroom, slow and lingering, and then leaves with another of his bright smiles.

I slip into a seat next to Grace, as usual, but we barely have time to say hello before Mr. Gaouette starts talking. She angles her notebook toward me and scribbles *How's it going?*

Good, I write in the corner of mine.

She narrows her eyes. *How's it actually going?*

I hesitate, pen hovered over my notebook. *Idk Ok I guess.*

Tell me more.

Idk if I think they caught the right person.

Who do you think it was??

Liam.

No idea. All I know is when they took him away, I didn't feel relieved. More questions than answers. Don't get me wrong, he's def a creep, but he didn't confess to anything & I just feel like I need some kinda actual closure before I really feel safe again. I'm being dumb, aren't I?

She shakes her head and pulls her notebook closer to herself, writing a long note before shoving it back toward me.

How you feel is legit whether he turns out guilty or innocent. Don't ever second guess your instincts. Better to be worried & safe than overconfident and dead. You don't have to feel relieved just because that's easier for everyone else. This didn't happen to them, it happened to you. & I'm always around if you wanna talk, you know that (I hope).

Grace . . . *gets* it. She's always understood me, maybe better than anyone. It's probably why I feel the way I do about her. Why every time I talk to her or see her or think about her, I question what I'm doing with Liam instead of Grace. The answer to the question is always the same, though. Grace is one of my best friends. Risking the loss of that friendship . . . it's a huge gamble.

I draw a big heart on my notebook paper and then set to work thoroughly crossing out everything I've written so no one else can see it if I accidentally leave this notebook open somewhere. Grace smiles at me and does the same.

And for a fleeting moment, I feel a little bit better than just okay.

26

Thursday night, Mom sits Hunter and me down at the table with her Serious Face on.

"I want to talk to you both about something," she says. "And I want to be clear that you can absolutely say no, okay?"

We both nod.

"Your dad and I got invited to a wedding this weekend in Massachusetts. We weren't going to go because of, well, you know. But with Calvin Omerton in jail right now waiting for his trial . . . We'd have to be there overnight on Saturday, but we'd be back early Sunday. What do you guys think?"

"I don't care if you go," says Hunter. "Whatever Amelia thinks is fine by me."

I am not fine with it. But I don't want to tell them that, because all my bad feelings are based on absolutely nothing, and my parents have been forced to revolve their lives around me for months. "I think you should go."

"You sure?" Mom's eyes pierce into my very soul.

"Yes. One hundred percent."

"Okay. Great." She grins broadly. "We'll go, then."

As soon as she frees us, I go up to my bedroom, a plan—possibly a very bad plan—forming in my mind. I slip my phone out of my pocket and text Liam. My parents will be away overnight this weekend. What should we do??

His response is almost immediate. I have a really great idea, actually. But you'll have to trust me.

Ooh, intrigue . . .

I'll pick you up Saturday morning around 10?? I promise, it'll be a great surprise. Such a great surprise. 😊

Sounds perfect.

And then I set down my phone, thinking hard. Maybe this is going to be a romantic surprise. Or maybe it's going to be a deadly one. I can't shake the horrible feeling in my gut that it could be either, and Grace told me to trust my gut. I want to talk about this with my friends, but I'm not sure that I can. Roman has been close with Liam for a long time, and I don't want him to feel uncomfortable. And Tera's his girlfriend, so, same. I hear voices downstairs—Skylar saying something to my mom—and then I hear her footsteps coming up. Used to be, she would stop in my room first, but I burned that bridge pretty thoroughly. It makes my heart hurt a little to think about how I lashed out at her, and at Hunter. It was a little bit about Liam, but it was more about jealousy over how much time she spends with my brother.

I cross the hall and knock on Hunter's door. He opens it and scowls at me.

"Want something?" he asks.

"Yeah, to apologize."

He lets me in. Sky's sitting on his bed, totally comfortable there.

"I just wanted to say that when I yelled at you, it wasn't really about Liam, and I shouldn't have yelled at you."

"What *was* it about?" Sky asks. Her voice is edged. She doesn't forgive me yet.

"It was about . . . well, you two. Don't get me wrong, I'm fine with you dating, and I know it doesn't matter if I am or I'm not, anyway. But you've been . . . I don't know, I feel like I never see you anymore, Sky. Like you want to be spending all your time with Hunter instead."

"You have a new boyfriend, too, Amelia. You don't think you've abandoned me at all in favor of him? I mean look how you reacted when Hunter tried to tell you what happened to make him hate Liam. You totally sided with your boyfriend over your family."

I feel defensive now and I wish I hadn't come in here. "I didn't side with Liam, I just felt . . . attacked. I don't know how I feel about Liam right now. Maybe he did kill those squirrels and maybe I *should* be careful with him, but maybe I shouldn't, and that's for *me* to figure out. I appreciate that you told me, but I don't like that you waited until a moment when you could spring it on me so aggressively, and you did it together like a pair of stern parents."

"And *you* should have said all of this to begin with." Sky

folds her arms. "Best friends should always be honest with each other. They shouldn't hold it in and then explode out of nowhere and then give each other the silent treatment and then come give a non-apology."

"You're right," I say, my throat thick with sorrow. "I guess we're not best friends."

And I walk out.

I don't know what's wrong with me. Why I can't swallow my pride and tell her I messed up and that I want to test if Liam is trustworthy, to figure it out once and for all. I can't trust that she and Hunter won't go straight to my parents and tell them everything, and I don't want that. I got myself into this, and I need to get myself out of it, one way or the other.

There is one person who can help me, though. I just don't want to get her *too* involved.

Hey can I ask you a weird favor? I text Grace.

Obv is her reply.

I'm gonna send you a link to a GPS tracking app. Download it and accept me as a friend on it? Just for the weekend. Everything's fine but I'm feeling super paranoid & I just want to be able to text someone if anything weird happens. Then the police will be able to find me. That sounds dramatic huh? I promise everything is ok other than my paranoia.

I send that, the link, and then a second text: Me & Sky are fighting.

It takes a while for her to reply, and I think maybe I pushed too far. Maybe this is too much to ask of someone without giving more details. But finally:

Ok I DL'd the app. I think we're friends on it now lol. I hope you know this is super weird Amelia. And I'm sorry about you and Sky. Hope it's over soon. ♥

Thx. I know It's weird. I'm not trying to be cagey. There's just honestly nothing to tell, I'm literally being paranoid.

Well I want you to feel and be safe no matter what. And I trust you.

She trusts me. I hold the phone to my chest, smiling.

No matter what happens or doesn't happen, I think Saturday is going to be terrible. But I'll get through it, and I know Grace is here for me, and that's something.

27

When Liam picks me up Saturday morning, I immediately feel like a jerk. What if I'm wrong to be suspicious of him? The more they search through Mr. Omerton's house, the more disgusting he turns out to be. He deserves to be in jail whether he murdered anyone or not. I was not safe living across the street from him, that's for sure. Mom has been absolutely beside herself about it.

Liam leans over to kiss my cheek, and I force a smile. Act natural. Guilty or innocent, Liam can't suspect that I'm unsure.

That thought twists a knot in my stomach. I have to break up with him. Not now, not today. But you can't date someone if you even have the *thought* that they might have tried to kill you. It's an unrecoverable thing. I think back over the past few months, how much fun we've had together. He's been so supportive, so kind, so wonderful. I slip my hand into his as he pulls out of my driveway.

Today we find out, I guess, if he's a monster, or if I am.

When we reach the town hall, Liam turns left toward Hen Falls.

"Where are we going?" I ask. Is that a tremor in my voice? Usually, I'd be so down for a surprise. But today I wish I knew exactly where he was taking me.

"I told you, it's a surprise," he says. "But fine, I can't wait to tell you any longer. My dad has a hunting camp up on one of the back roads, and I thought we could hang out there, have a romantic day. There's a fireplace, so we won't freeze. Only thing is my dad doesn't trust strangers to go up there. So he'll meet us there, but he won't stay long. You've been wanting to anyway, haven't you? You wanted to meet him."

"Oh, well, yeah, of course." I am so not ready to meet his crappy dad today. Nervously, I smooth my shirt—just a plain, light blue V-neck. My jacket's tossed in the back seat. "Is what I'm wearing okay?"

"Trust me, he's not going to have a problem with your outfit."

I force a laugh. "What *will* he have a problem with?"

His laugh sounds real. "It's not *you* he hates. He'll be perfectly nice to you. I promise."

"Okay." Something about this feels *very* wrong. Maybe it's not. Maybe it's fine.

I spend ten minutes telling myself it's fine, making light small talk with Liam, but the longer we're in this car, the more not-fine this feels.

Somethings off. Pls don't reply just get help. GPS on & I'm ok rn. Going to Liams camp.

I send the text to Grace and then delete it immediately and pretend to be scrolling through Instagram, making sure he sees me comment on a couple of pictures so he thinks that's what I was doing in the first place. This was a bad idea, such a bad idea. What made me think I should get in a car with Liam when for days my mind has been cycling around all the things that scare me about him?

My arms feel numb and weak, so I set down my phone before my nerves become visible.

"Anything good?" he asks.

"Nah, just a bunch of selfies as usual."

"That's why I avoid social media," he says, expression sour.

"Oh, come on. We'll get you posting more, eventually. People enjoy seeing your face, you know."

His expression warms. "We'll see."

Even though I told Grace not to reply to my text, part of me wishes she had. Not knowing what I'm walking into or if anyone will be able to help me is utterly terrifying. I want to call Mom right now and beg them to come back from that wedding. But it's too late for that. I've already made my bed.

Liam's tires crunch as he turns onto a snow-covered side road. I've been out this way before, I think. It's pretty barren, minus the hunting camps, but maybe I could use the forest to my advantage, if I had to. Liam might be the more athletic of the two of us, but I'm a good, fast runner, and I've spent a lot of time in the woods. He turns up another road, his tires skidding a little on the icy underlayer. Neither of us comments on the lack of fresh tire tracks, the fact that no one's been in or out since we got snow. I consider leaping out, making a run for it, but something tells me that wouldn't end well for me.

I'm eerily calm, considering that I've basically allowed myself to become a hostage. My palms are sweaty, but my mind was at least partly prepared for this. The only thing I'm worried about is whether his dad actually is up here. Are they working as a team? I can't do anything about the two of them together. Liam alone is stronger than me.

Liam parks the car outside a small log structure, a fairly typical hunting camp. "There's no smoke rising," he says. "You'll want your coat till we get a fire going."

Dutifully, I reach into the back seat to retrieve it. He waits till I start putting it on, then gets out of the car while I'm tugging my arms into the sleeves. He opens my door for me and holds out his hand. I wipe mine discreetly on my jeans before taking his and zip my phone into my coat pocket with the other.

When Liam opens the door of the hunting camp, a foul smell bursts out at me. Oh. *Oh.*

He pushes me inside with a hand on the small of my back, then closes the door and leans against it. Wide gaps in the logs plus high windows on all sides of the cabin provide plenty of light, and honestly, I wish they didn't. Because lying in the middle of the floor is a mostly decomposed body. A skeleton nearly bared, with leathered skin still clinging around the ribs and chest. The sight—and smell—makes me gag.

"Amelia, meet my father," says Liam, and there's laughter in his voice. "I thought you two might get along. You like bugs and, well, their larvae sure like him."

"You did this?" I whisper. I don't even know what else to say or do or think. It was one thing to consider it in the dark safety of my room: *I think my boyfriend is a killer*. It's another thing to see it before my very eyes. To see what he did to *his own father*. To know, without a doubt, that he plans to do the same thing to me.

The thought is so chilling, so bone-deep terrifying, it freezes me entirely.

"It was actually an accident. He tripped over a branch trying to chase me down, hit his head on the tailgate of his truck. His skull cracked open like an egg." Liam's eyes flash with a darkness I have never seen in them before. He's haunted by whatever his father did to him before this moment, but that doesn't make any of it okay. "But seeing him lying there, lifeless, it reminded me that there's a really good way to take care of your enemies."

"Was Maria your enemy? And Lydia?"

He shrugs. "No. And neither were you. You're not stupid; you know it's the brothers I want to suffer. Otherwise I think I would have made the deaths much slower. The only mistake I made was not checking to make sure *you* were actually dead. Because it wasn't Hunter who suffered after that, was it? It was you." He tilts his head pensively. "Honestly, Amelia, I enjoyed dating you. I didn't think that I would. I thought you were kind of . . . weird. But you're not, really. I actually like you a lot, I think. Maybe that's why I let this go on so long."

Tears burn hot in my eyes. It'd be easier if he'd just told me he hated me. "Then why do this? Why not just let me go?"

He scoffs. "A little late now, don't you think? You know too much. You've seen my dad, and you've— Besides, you weren't going to keep on dating me anyway, were you? You like that girl, Grace, don't you? She's next, by the way." His eyes glint. Jealousy.

"I don't get it. I can understand, if your father— If you felt like he deserved it. But I don't understand how you could kill someone who hasn't hurt you and feel—feel *fine* about it. Why, Liam?"

"You don't have to understand. It was a means to an end. The killing was the means, watching the brothers suffer was the end. The rest . . ." He shrugs again. "I feel nothing about it."

"Nothing?"

"Nothing." He takes a step closer. "Is this enough closure for you? Because I'm starting to get bored."

"No," I say, panicked. "This is *not* enough closure for me." Another step.

"I won't tell a soul, Liam. Just let me go. Let me live. I will stay with you forever if you want. I'll marry you, I'll live with you, I'll let you—"

I can't finish the sentence, even though in this moment I

feel like I would let him kill a thousand women if it meant he would leave me alive.

Liam chuckles, amused by my fear. "Oh, Amelia. There is no promise you can make that'd convince me to let you live, not now. That's the thing about people who are alive: They can promise anything, but they're almost always liars."

"I'm not." My voice is hoarse. I back up toward the far wall, trying to put as much space between us as possible even though it doesn't matter.

"No? How many times did you say you were going to let this go? I sent those texts, by the way, if you didn't figure it out. I liked how worked up it made you, and I was curious if you would actually heed my warnings."

"That's *different*. That's before I *knew*. I—"

"Spare me." He doesn't say it with anger. His voice is perfectly even, calm, like we're having a regular conversation. "Just so you know, I would have killed you either way. I just didn't want you to figure it out beforehand. And don't worry, I'll do this right. It's like you said the other day, *we don't know what the killer does with boyfriends*. You'll wind up dead, and I'll wind up injured, and the police won't know *what* to do."

"They'll figure it out," I say hoarsely. But it'll be too late for me when they do.

"You haven't told anyone where we are, have you?"

I shake my head.

"You sure? Let me see your phone."

I don't want to give him my phone, my lifeline, but I also

don't want him to come any nearer. I fish it out of my pocket, unlock it, and toss it to him, hoping with everything in my soul that no one's texted me. Other than the deleted texts to Grace, I haven't put a word of my suspicions in writing, but I don't like the thought of him going through my messages nonetheless. As if I didn't feel vulnerable enough. Whatever he finds there, it seems to satisfy him. He slams the phone hard on the floor and I watch it shatter. And now . . . what's next? His eyes meet mine, and I know what's next.

"You know, I'm not going to make this easy," I say, even though I'm not sure my limbs can move.

He doesn't even respond. Simply meanders closer. So casual. "This part is new to me. The part where I can see the fear in your eyes. The others never saw me coming."

"And does the fear make it better or worse?"

If I can keep him talking, maybe, *maybe*, help will come in time.

He grins slowly, and I can't stand how handsome he looks while he's being such a monster. So compelling and repulsive at once. So easily able to slide into the regular world like he isn't hiding a blood-smeared soul.

"You weren't so clever as you think, you know," I say, because suddenly I want to make him angry. I want to see him react to something like a normal person would. Like I would have thought *he* would, before today. "Just because I didn't tell anyone doesn't mean I didn't figure it out."

There it is. The smallest flash, but it's definitely anger in his eyes.

"And you know what? Other people are going to figure it out, too."

He reaches me in two strides. "Too bad for you, you won't be around to see it."

I duck under his arm, and I've reached the door before he realizes it. I throw it open and bolt outside. I sprint down the path we drove up, but I stay near the side in case he gets in his car. It's slippery—brutal early winter ice hidden under the thin layer of snow. Treacherous. But if I don't run, I'm dead. So I keep going. He's catching up to me, though. I'm fast, but he's faster.

Right as he's about to catch me, I make a bold move. Let my foot slip on the ice, fall hard on my back. My head slams against the ground, my glasses skitter away, and black spots swim across my vision. Liam skids to a halt, but he slips, too.

I flip over and try to crawl to my feet, but he grabs onto my foot, yanking me toward him. I kick out with my other foot, and it connects with his face. Hard enough that he calls me a terrible name but not hard enough to do any real damage. I grasp desperately for anything that could help me—a stick, a rock, *anything*—but he has both my feet in his grip now and he's dragging me toward the middle of the road, away from anything I can use.

"This was fun," he snarls. "But it's over now."

When I try to writhe out of his grip, he punches me hard in the ribs. My body curls involuntarily, like a pill bug playing dead. And before I can do anything else, I'm pinned to the ground with a knife pressed against my throat.

I have never held so utterly still.

He smiles, so broadly. And then, the sound of tires squealing.

Liam looks up. His weight shifts, and I take my chance. Pull my knee up as hard as I can into his crotch.

It works, at least well enough for me to get free. The sounds of an approaching vehicle get louder, but I don't have time to wait and be rescued. I grab a big tree branch, and I swing. It cracks against Liam's side, but he's wild now, desperate. He slices a deep gash in my arm with his knife and gets hold of the end of my branch. He shoves it hard into my stomach, sending pain ratcheting through my already injured ribs, but I don't let go. I can't.

A truck appears then and slams into Liam. He flies up over the hood, falls off the back of the vehicle, and lies still in the road.

It's Sky in her dad's truck.

She leaps out of the driver's seat, a lacrosse stick in one hand, and looms cautiously over Liam's still form. I join her, even more cautiously.

"Is he dead?" I whisper.

"No, definitely not." Sky prods him with the lacrosse stick. "But he's unconscious. Hang on, I'm pretty sure Dad keeps duct tape in here. We'll make sure he can't move if he wakes up."

She hands me the lacrosse stick and I hold it in both hands, shivering, my head spinning, while Sky hauls herself into the bed of the truck and opens the toolbox. She's so calm while she wraps Liam's arms and legs in layer upon layer of duct tape. It makes me even less calm, somehow.

When she's done, I collapse onto the ground and start to cry.

Sky sits beside me but doesn't touch me. "Are you hurt?"

"I don't know," I manage between gasping sobs. "I think a little."

She rests a hand on my back, firm and anchoring. "The police are on their way. Probably an ambulance, too. And your parents are coming home from the wedding. Everything's okay now. Everything is going to be fine."

"How are you so *calm*?" I scream it, because I've never been further from calm.

"I'm not." Her voice has an edge for the first time. "Amelia, I just watched you nearly killed and I'm   I don't know what to say or what to do, I just—"

I hug her tight and cry even harder.

"Grace called me," she says, answering the question I don't have the breath to ask. "After she called the police. She was terrified they wouldn't get to you in time, because they had to come get her phone to use the tracking app. I think she hoped my parents or your parents could do something, but they're all headed to that stupid wedding." Her arm tightens, just slightly. "And when she said that you told her you'd be at Liam's camp . . . well, I knew where that was, so I decided to do something about it. It was stupid, coming up here all by myself. Such a terrible, terrible idea. But I'm glad I did. Hunter's headed to the dam; he thought the text you sent Grace was probably from Liam, to throw us off, and that he took you to the dam instead of here. I should text Hunter, right? So he knows you're alive and okay."

"Yeah, you should text him."

She doesn't make a move for her phone yet. "You tried to tell us you were worried about him, didn't you? The other night when you came to apologize."

I nod.

"I shouldn't have yelled at you. I should have done all of this better. I'm just— I *did* abandon you a little bit, and I was ashamed of that, so I didn't handle it very well."

"Stop," I say weakly. "I handled it all wrong, too. I love you and I'm sorry."

"I love you and I'm sorry, too."

I wipe fiercely at my eyes and look up at her. "I would have died, Skylar. The only reason I'm not dead right now is that he got distracted when he heard the sound of your dad's truck. You saved my life."

Her eyes are filled with tears now, which her rapid blinking doesn't begin to hide. I bury my face in her clavicle again, and she rests her chin on my head.

"He can't hurt you now," she says, and in the background I hear the faint sound of sirens. "He will never hurt you again."

28

I do not like the hospital. It doesn't matter how many McFlurries and fries Aunt Jenna sneaks in for me, nor how much extra attention I get because she works here; it doesn't make it any better. I have broken ribs and stitches in my arm, neither of which are worthy of an overnight stay. But there's also the concussion, which they're worried about because of my barely healed previous concussion, so I'm here for three days while they monitor me. It's better to be safe—I know that. But all I want is to go home. I've spent way too much time in this hospital already, and if I never see it again it'll be too soon.

I've seen nearly everyone. My parents drove home from Massachusetts so fast, they're lucky they didn't get arrested. Hunter and Sky have barely left my room. Sky's parents have come, and Tera and her mom, and Roman and his parents. My grandparents. Detective Cheney. Almost everyone I could possibly want to see, and then some.

And then, after school on Monday, Grace visits. Roman

drives her, but he and Tera disappear to the hospital cafeteria the second they arrive.

"Sorry I didn't come sooner," Grace says, pacing slowly next to my bed. "I was . . . scared to see you."

"Why?"

She shrugs sheepishly. Gestures to my bandaged arm. "I felt . . . I didn't like the idea of you hurt again, of you almost dying again. You look okay, though." She pauses, smiling apologetically as though she realizes how uncomplimentary that is. "You look good."

"Thanks." I nestle deeper into my pillow. "I should not have put you in the position I did without telling you I was suspicious of Liam. I didn't think about how much danger I was getting into, and how much responsibility I was putting on *you*. I thought I could manipulate him more than he manipulated me. Why did I think that?"

"It's okay." She sits on a stool next to the bed, reaches for my hand. "You're alive and relatively well, and he's behind bars. Maybe it wasn't a good idea. Probably it wasn't. But it doesn't matter now. All that matters is how it turned out."

"Are you trying to tell me the ends justify the means?"

She laughs. "That's a dangerous assertion. Next time, why don't you go ahead and not attempt vigilante justice."

It's my turn to laugh. "I think that's best. I don't seem cut out for it. Without Sky . . ." I shudder. "I'm really, really glad you called her."

"Me too." She frowns. "But wow, you small-town people are impulsive."

"It may not be impulsiveness so much as it is an arrogant belief that we can take care of ourselves no matter what." Her hand's still around mine, and I squeeze her fingers. "I should have— Even during the parts where I thought Liam was a great boyfriend, I shouldn't have been with him."

She swallows audibly. "Then why were you?"

"I was scared." It's harder to admit than I thought it would be. "I didn't want to lose you as a friend if things . . . you know."

"Worst-case planning. Very practical."

"Practical, yeah. But also kind of stupid."

"I don't know. That day when you told me how you felt, I could have chased you down. I think maybe that would have been all the difference. Would've stopped you dating a serial killer, at least. I hope."

"Well, I guess *dated a serial killer* is a more interesting legacy than *accidentally fell off a cliff*, right? Even if it makes me feel like a complete moron in retrospect." I grin at her, and she grins back. I try to move closer to the edge of the bed, but my ribs absolutely kill, and my smile turns into a grimace.

"Don't," she says. She reaches out a hand to stop me trying to move, and I pretty much don't even breathe. She sits carefully on the side of the hospital bed. Brushes hair away from my face. "So, what are you thinking . . . practical, or impractical?"

"My breath is kind of terrible," I say, because now that she's so near me, I'm pretty nervous.

"I don't care." There's laughter in her voice. Her mouth is so near mine.

"Impractical," I whisper, and she kisses me.

I know at once that it's the right thing. My life is messy, and there are some hard things ahead. I'm going to have to testify against Liam when his case goes to trial. I'll have to face whatever punishment I get from Mom and Dad, and I'll have to deal with the memories of what happened for the rest of my life.

But it's okay, because I'm alive, and Liam can't hurt me or anyone else ever again. He'll be locked away till the day he dies. I have the best family and friends, and I have Grace.

I'm going to be just fine.

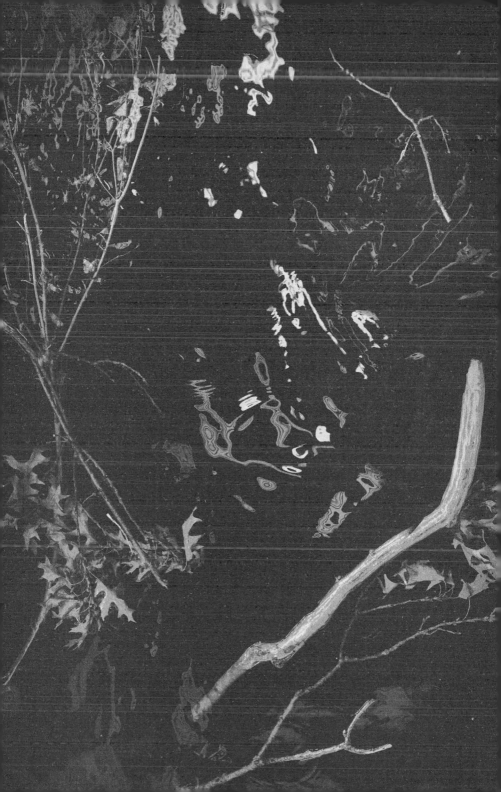

ACKNOWLEDGMENTS

I am so grateful to my editor, Amanda Maciel, for her wisdom and guidance through our third(!) book together. Also to Talia Seidenfeld and everyone else at Scholastic who has helped work on this book. It takes a lot to get a novel from a rough draft manuscript to a finished product, and I'm so appreciative of the help I've received through every step.

My agent, Sarah LaPolla, has been right there with me through pretty much all the ups and downs I've had in this career. I would most definitely not be where I am today without her.

There's no better support system when you're writing a book than other authors. I'm particularly grateful to Somaiya Daud, Laurie Devore, Maurene Goo, Kate Hart, Michelle Krys, Amy Lukavics, Veronica Roth, Michelle Schusterman, Courtney Summers, and Kara Thomas for all their help and cheering on while I worked on this book.

I would be remiss if I didn't mention my coworkers at Pete and Gerry's, especially my T2 companions, and *especially*

especially, Heather Cheney. I couldn't ask for anyone better to share an office with than Heather, who listens to all my opinions (of which I have many) and has somehow not gotten bored of me yet.

My family has been supportive since the beginning. My parents, Denis and Jeanne Ward. My sister, Jackie Ward. Tyler, Abel, and Quinn Gaouette. Elaine Millett. Andrea, Roger, and Maren Marecaux. My husband, Brandon Millett, and my son, Michael.

And as ever, I am grateful to readers. Without you, I wouldn't get to do this dream job. Thank you so much for reading my stories.

Kaitlin Ward is the author of the YA novels *Where She Fell, Girl in a Bad Place,* and *Bleeding Earth.* She grew up on a dairy farm in a tiny New Hampshire town, the same town where she lives now with her husband and son. Find her on Twitter at @Kaitlin_Ward.

Also by Kaitlin Ward